*"**Some Things Are Better Left to Saxophones** is terrific, both in the colloquial sense and the root meaning of the word."*

—Stephen Brill, Professor of English literature and film studies at Wayne State University

CRITICAL PRAISE FOR EARLIER WORK

WHAT WAITING REALLY MEANS

This witty little book skitters nervously from topic to topic, recording Mary's clever apercus, chronicaling her odd habits, and cataloguing her obsessive dreams ... a britle first novel that amuses with every crack.

—Kirkus Reviews

IS THIS WHAT OTHER WOMEN FEEL TOO?

Seese's voice is tough, lyrical and darkly funny ... her writing is fragmented but engaging, and the cleverness of it is that you can't always tell the wisdom from the wisecracks.

—Detroit Free Press

JAMES MASON AND THE WALK-IN CLOSET

There is a kind of bad news that goes far beyond the serial killings or the neglected children or the brush fires or the black ice that we read about every day ... June Akers Seese is the mistress of what is probably a universal female sorrow. The women in these 13 stories have been alienated from conventional roles, but remain unliberated by the feminist move-

ment, and are thereby stranded in silent anguish between 2 worlds, belonging to neither. The woman in the title novella states: "I don't pretend to understand my life. I sleep with a defrocked priest and work for a man who likes boys. There's then and now. Then I lived in Scottsdale. Now I live in Dublin. Then I had a job and the Irishman and what passed for an ordinary life. Now I have what's left."

—Washington Post Book World

Some Things Are Better Left to Saxophones

SOME THINGS ARE BETTER LEFT TO SAXOPHONES

A Novel

June Akers Seese

iUniverse, Inc.
New York Lincoln Shanghai

Some Things Are Better Left to Saxophones

Copyright © 2007 by June Akers Seese

All rights reserved. No part of this book may be used or reproduced by any means, graphic, electronic, or mechanical, including photocopying, recording, taping or by any information storage retrieval system without the written permission of the publisher except in the case of brief quotations embodied in critical articles and reviews.

iUniverse books may be ordered through booksellers or by contacting:

iUniverse
2021 Pine Lake Road, Suite 100
Lincoln, NE 68512
www.iuniverse.com
1-800-Authors (1-800-288-4677)

Because of the dynamic nature of the Internet, any Web addresses or links contained in this book may have changed since publication and may no longer be valid.

This is a work of fiction. All of the characters, names, incidents, organizations, and dialogue in this novel are either the products of the author's imagination or are used fictitiously.

Cover design by Sandra Commito

ISBN: 978-0-595-44661-2 (pbk)
ISBN: 978-0-595-69080-0 (cloth)
ISBN: 978-0-595-88984-6 (ebk)

Printed in the United States of America

For Sandy Commito, who knows there's more to chicken soup than the noodles and the bone.

Acknowledgments

I would like to thank the corporation of Yaddo where most of this novel was written, as well as Ann Davis of the Georgia Council for the Arts for her ongoing support of my fiction. My thanks also go to Anne Feldman, for her love and encouragement. I would be remiss if I did not include Perry Gray Seese; and once again, Pearl Cleage, Agi Hebebrand, and Lois Nichols, my friends to the grave. I appreciate, too, the late night talks with Barbara Stacks, Jackie Marashi, Karen Moore and Victoria Korson. A final thanks to Eric Robert Kuhne who shares my distaste for clichés and who, more than once, has saved my life.

CHAPTER 1

I have a retarded daughter who rolls silverware in big white hotel napkins downtown. She rides the Detroit bus to and from her job, gets off at Grand Circus Park, and because she is pretty and smiles a lot we worry about those weekday bus rides, my husband, Charlie and I. So far, so good, but luck has a lot to do with it and after age 65 we don't feel so lucky. Detroit has never been a lucky place, even for those who grew rich here. Henry Ford ran out of luck when his anti-Semitism caught up with him; and Father Coughlin ran out of luck too when President Roosevelt took him off the air for the same brand of hate. Detroit is a city of immigrants, whether from Poland or South Georgia, who thought the assembly line was an answer. A chance to work hard and prosper. That's what our family tried to do too. But we did not plan to end up avoiding each other.

Let me set a few things straight and keep them that way: I have to hang onto something tight in order to endure what has come my way. Not grammar with its book-sure use of the "ly" ending. Not even the *New Yorker*, though we still subscribe. Charlie's an English teacher, and I have not yet given up on Hilton Als or Jeffrey Toobin, although the other writers are mediocre; for the magazine has lost its substance and style in a sea of gloss. It is even hard to hang on to your friends, though I keep on through divorces and deaths and relocations. Master of a thank you note on Crane's best engraved note cards and perfect offbeat gifts—that's me. I wrap my offerings in newspaper and mash hot pink bows on top, but that's hardly original and certainly not as thrifty as it seems; yet I hate to be overlooked and these gifts stand out in a crowd. It's also possible that one friend drifted on because she got scared watching our lives pull away from the bone. I don't dwell on that possibility.

I've managed to stick with Charlie for forty-six years, but there have been times when we both visited a divorce attorney: he in person, and me over the phone for a lunch hour jam of questions that could have continued past sunset; but we both considered our options. Alone, how could we handle Melody and the fools she encounters? We looked around at other splits and soon came to our senses. The divorce arrangements we watched floated above the confessional and bypassed common sense. They made the word "lie" have a million variations including a new wardrobe for the ex-wife who is supposed to cast off her old life, and a part-time job that's supposed to mean something. Well, it does. It means she doesn't have insurance or a vacation unless she finagles one. And it means she has four less hours to worry through. No thanks. I already have work enough and can live in the clothes I have. They cost enough the first time around, and we don't go so many places that I need cruise wear or $200 hiking boots.

As Charlie says, "The idea is you get a new spouse who hasn't shared all that pain and can be a manager, not a mother, and there are four of you then, if you're civilized, to share the work!" It's a bitter remark, but true in marriages I've seen break as clean as a brazil nut at Christmas—not the sort you smash to bits; the kind where someone knows how to wield the nutcracker.

Yes, I needed a husband to split the trips to the many doctors; the long drives to find playmates, the outings that went nowhere. Some parents want their offspring to associate with "normal" kids for soccer and Sunday school, especially if their retarded child doesn't look "funny." A few parents are retarded too and thus live with a grandmother. Imagine those two generations in one house! Imagine growing old and waiting for death with the caretaker role reversed. I don't think too long about that possibility either. Appearance means more than it should to all of us. Retardation is every day; and it sounds cloying to summarize moments that save you, that enable you to laugh, and stop laughing before you can't stop yourself; but these moments were usually spent with Charlie.

When we all lived under one roof and tried too hard to help each other, I made mistakes. Sometimes I understand why John Baxter moved to Alaska. In those days I'd take him and the others to the Detroit Zoo and give them freedom while I kept track of Melody. Too much freedom. They would have given it a different name back then. The zoo seemed safe with its fences and guards and crackerjack sellers working their way through college. Indeed Melody was safe, for our eyes never left her. I sacrificed the others for her and regret it now.

Then I would have needed an obvious alternative and someone with a mouth like a jackhammer to pound some sense into my head. There was no alternative, though I spent years looking for one, and all along my children exuded a softness that I absorbed like lip balm. They were masters of restraint until they graduated from high school. Maybe they were afraid of me—my short fuse—my fierce political opinions. In those days Charlie would just walk away when I was raving about Watergate and later take me with him: "You need a few turns around the block," he'd say and we'd move through the sunset on the Huntington Woods sidewalks where we have walked together for forty years. I'd like to say this neighborhood was a solace, because it is to many, but I was boiling inside then, and Charlie was the only solace I had.

His hands, his eyes, the sight of him bending over and ferociously shining his shoes or knotting his tie, his white shirt stiff from the cleaners, his themes ready to record and return. He's a fastidious man and the only thing he has kept too long is his briefcase, past the point of cracked leather and bulging sides. Charlie was fond of quoting Mark Twain whenever I told him he had to relax. I could handle Saturdays alone.

"Golf, Charlie?"

"Golf is a good walk, spoiled," was his offering to me as he walked out the door in the sun of a weekend morning.

"Tennis is a status symbol gone berserk," I countered.

"Who said that?" he replied.

"I did."

He'd snap my bottom as he passed. That sign of affection just revved me up.

"Have some fun. Instead of listening to bigots rationalize their country club dues."

"I'm playing at a public court," he said slowly.

I couldn't see the look on Charlie's face because the screen door had already slammed, but this weekend banter was trivial.

Thinking that work would be our salvation, we threw ourselves into the dying public school system and its battles in order to feel part of something that might work. Far enough away from a mind that had stopped growing at the age of ten, not *slowed up*, *stopped*. And not *challenged*. Death of the mind—only we still had the whole person to protect and steer through the maze of illusory benefits provided by our government and school system. And we had her body with its gait that might have been seen as tipsy in a normal girl. We had a beauty with thick curls and a wide smile for all.

In the early years, my husband and I were a team. I'd blow into the Special Ed office with the horrific details of the latest mainstream fiasco, and he'd be the voice of reason; far angrier than I, but always with the threat or presence of his lawyer. They listened to him: "No job like you promised? So keep her an extra six months." Suddenly we discovered an ex-nun and the world of job coaches, who change faster than I can blink on days when I twitch as well as cry. And all of these battles were fought and won at the expense of our other children who had too much housework, for too long, beginning too soon. Order meant too much to me.

My children grew to hate lists, but they did the chores, and on time, because they knew how hard it was for us; how we at least never succumbed to TV trays, vegetarianism, or eating fast food alone in front of game shows or at a sticky kitchen counter. I kept them close and busy so they couldn't escape into school activities. They were all too good and lied to me too—dragging Melody along—when it suited me and drowned their social lives. I was blind to what was happening until they had all gone as far away as possible: Japan, Alaska, a seedy boardinghouse on the WSU campus. You think we have big family holidays now? We have phone calls and postcards, plenty of them; but our children are lost. Furthermore, not one married. It's more than genetic worry. Teenagers should rebel. Ours didn't. They might argue over a bike or beg for car keys, but that was all. Now they pretend Melody will be off their backs when we die, that group homes aren't setups for abuse, and that independent living is independent.

Our son in Alaska, John Baxter, even believes that Melody can survive with a paid companion who comes monthly to balance her checkbook in an apartment with a roommate. Don't get me started on these pseudo solutions. You need to hear how we got to this point. We started out as upbeat idealists. In America, things can be fixed. We never thought to look beneath that assumption until we had to. I felt lucky then. Other husbands left. Other women ate anti-depressants, some actually went nuts. Others got jobs they didn't want and found a bedroom for a grandmother who watched TV all day after the mini-bus left at dawn. One woman just slept too late one morning.

CHAPTER 2

The best advice, the single sentence that sticks, came from a tall, red-faced shrink about to retire, "If you can't change something, get the fuck away from it." He could have just mouthed a pamphlet: "Vacations are …" But he knew the force of words and how fast we were sinking. So we took his advice. We went to my favorite city, New York. Until I got married at 25, I had no urge to go anywhere else. In those days, you could drive a Ford there, deliver it, and the ride was free. I traveled with friends and we laughed and made lists all the way to the Connecticut Turnpike. Free or cheap, not just the Staten Island Ferry and the benches in Central Park. Even free Shakespeare with long lines; but when you're together, the lines can become an outdoor cocktail party.

We stayed with other friends who had already moved there. In those days, we drank rotgut or vodka, and some of the men carried half-pints in their pockets. We were soft-spoken once we left the car. I had lived three blocks from the Hancock Station through college at WSU and knew what the cops were capable of after a lame excuse like a missing sticker on your car window. Drinking in a public place, if you were loud enough, might get you into trouble. But my worries were groundless. New York's finest had other fish to fry, protesters, criminals. They knew better than to waste energy on talkers in line, be they college students or street people. I have always taken seriously Hemingway's admonition: "Anything goes, but keep your eye out for the policeman around the corner." I never took a drug stronger than codeine-laced cough syrup. Alcohol was enough then. Keep it legal. Keep it simple, I thought. I'd read Thoreau and tried to make his words part of my life.

So New York remained my town and it made sense to return. Charlie took me there gladly. We had romance all right and rest—for one night. He had waited too long to take the shrink's advice, and ended up the second day with pneumonia at Lenox Hill Hospital. Charlie couldn't fly home with pneumonia, and after he fainted while going to the toilet, he paid attention to what the doctor said and slept on and on. I walked through some snow banks and brought him back a bathrobe we couldn't afford and a jar of African violets that lasted the week we were there.

It was the week Anne Baxter died. Jackie O. came to visit her. Outside the hospital window, trees stood as elegant as those thin trees on Park Avenue and the snow was soft and steady. I sat and watched Charlie sleep, and in some ways it was a real vacation; just the two of us, no laundry or cooking. Melody wasn't there and I could snooze in the recliner next to Charlie's bed. I like hospital custard. Those hamburgers tasted like hamburgers and you could salt mashed potatoes without considering the risk of an early grave then. As for drink, who needed it? I was away and relaxed. So was Bobby Short, away, out of town, usually just around the block; but one night I went out and ate at the Carlyle alone anyway and sat below surely the biggest fresh floral arrangement in town. I took my time. Mood matters, even when the music dies. I bought Short's CD instead, and Charlie still has it and his Cole Porter book too.

My relaxation didn't last long when I found out my baby-sitter, a middle-aged blonde who kept dogs in Livonia, had to feed them daily. This little journey was over by rush hour. The real surprise was only human, but scared me bad. The sitter, lonely after the first week turned into two, brought in her boyfriend whose idea of breakfast was a cold Budweiser. I have a long, wide window in the kitchen and my neighbor gave me a report. "The guy works late hours, kiddo!" How much damage can he do? I thought. The sitter could have left me holding the bag; there are worse things and you better believe it. But the shrink's advice had somehow missed its mark by a mile and when I got home we had a big hospital bill and a daughter who asked for a dog at least ten times a day, all that spring. She took picture books of dogs out of the library in stacks, and she flipped through the pages and looked forlorn. I had enough to deal with without asking for more. Toilet train for a fifth time? She wanted a Sheepdog!

"Where will our next vacation take us?" I thought but didn't rub it in. I took the medicine the shrink gave me, free samples, and they worked. For a year or so I could sleep. Then he retired and the advice stopped, but he increased my dose before our last visit. His partner, a tall lanky man with curly hair and a southern accent looked like a redneck to me and I told him so. "Protective coloration," the new doctor replied. I like a man who can take a joke. So we continued to get help every Friday and it was worth its weight in gold. I needed more than medicine. I needed the truth and neither of these men were liars. They hated self-help books more than we did. They didn't work for the government or the school system, so we had our hour of reality on a weekly basis. We cursed and cried and laughed and kept on trying.

Finally we were left with nobody for our Friday mornings. "I need a referee to talk to you," my husband said with a wink. My fuse, away from my daughter, grew shorter with the years. Once someone asked me about the holes in the dining room walls. "That's where I kick on the lights. The builder drank and got the outlets too low!" Bending over seemed like a waste of time. When he was done and paid, I noticed his mistake. Eventually we bought patching plaster, new wallpaper, and a punching bag for me.

I grew shriveled. Long showers. Baths. I can still feel the relief of hot water from those years. The sounds first, then the steam, and finally, if I remembered to buy it, the bath oil. Candles scared me. Sure, I've seen their potential for romance in the tub, but burning the house down is a nightmare I have too often to risk flickering beauty and candle glow. A hotel bathrobe and the smell of lavender are enough for me. I'm an old-fashioned woman and succumb to a feather bed with enough down pillows to play with. After I leave the tub and the hair dryer, the bathroom door flies open. Sometimes I'm not too tired for love and my husband smiles as my head bends down.

Charlie and I met in the Miles Poetry Room at Wayne State. I went there to play a record of Tennessee Williams reading an outrageous story about a preacher's daughter who ended up in a New Orleans brothel. They had Faulkner reading his stories too—in his melodious Mississippi accent. And Dylan Thomas. Each man had a voice like no other, and I was drawn to the safety of the room. On this particular afternoon, I had just walked out of an

Edith Sitwell presentation—scared off by her grotesque head wrap and huge rings. She sat in a wheelchair; a tall woman of advanced years whose words meant nothing to me. The students on either side of my folding chair seemed in awe of her. I starred at her gnarled hands and beak-like nose and left fast.

I pulled Williams off the shelf and sank into a chair. I expected to be mercifully alone for an hour; but then classes changed and students dribbled in from the Sitwell reception. They were serving punch and cookies right outside the door. Charlie walked in with a plastic glass in his hand and smiled at me. Then he looked around and walked out without checking the shelves or even looking at the clock. I saw him again in a Studies Course in Henry James and Mark Twain. It was summer and the reading was voluminous. I had a full time job complete with overtime, so I had to drop the class after the third session and I didn't get my money back. Charlie commiserated with me at the break, but I still didn't know his name. Finally, I was sitting close to the door in Advanced Literary Criticism when he took the seat next to mine just as the bell rang. It became his seat three times a week. He copied my notes more than once, and then we started talking after class; but we never had so much as coffee until the course ended in December.

After the New Year, I got a call from him and we made a date to see *The Mouse That Roared*, a satiric film with plenty of black comedy. I hardly remember any of the plot because I spent the two hours thinking about what it would be like to kiss him. I found out soon enough. The winter semester took on a whole new dimension; we were engaged by April and we spent July and August in summer school. In September I made my way through the carnations at The Shrine of the Little Flower and listened to Charlie say, "I do." It all went so fast and the next day we left town. My Maid of Honor gave us a week at her mother's cottage at Houghton Lake, and the world seemed bent to the right shape.

    The furniture was rickety and we broke the day bed by the front door by just sitting on it. When a neighbor came by to collect the key, he grinned at the damage. Ironic, because our romance took place in the bedroom with the door closed. I soon memorized the arrangement of the logs on the ceiling. It was a simple routine: sleeping late, guzzling orange juice, writing thank you notes for our wedding gifts, and going out on the lake in a kayak Charlie had built. The lake was smooth, no waves; and I got sunburned in no time. We took a long nap every day. Charlie made bologna sandwiches for supper and we went back to bed with mustard on our lips. The last night we stood on the dock in the moonlight, and I wondered why I felt scared. The future, I guess, even then, resembled a dirt road. From the beginning, Charlie was the optimist in the family. He couldn't stop talking about our new apartment on campus: "It is a studio on the fourth floor, but the building has an elevator and it is furnished!"

CHAPTER 3

Charlie and I are teachers. Not in the same school system. I can walk to work. The Burton Elementary School is not far from our front door; but Huntington Woods doesn't have a high school, so my husband had to look further. Royal Oak is close enough and famous. Tom Hayden was spawned there and at least 80% of its students were still college bound. It was built in 1927 and has kept its image of solidity; having survived, early on, the Crash, the Depression, and World War II. Its arched doorways and windows are far from the street. Charlie has taught at Royal Oak-Dondero High School for forty years. Last year his load was three honors classes and two sessions of sophomore English—not the fast track, but the one where the reading lists are geared to working class hopefuls.

He makes a lab out of Mark Twain, and includes a CD of Hal Holbrook's one man show. The short stories crack us both up and we never get tired of the "The Stolen White Elephant," a satire on the police department that's as fresh now as when Twain wrote it. Ken Burns brought Twain to us at just the right time this year on TV, and his background music of the ups and downs of Twain's long life made sense to us and to Charlie's students as well. The fast track is another story and I don't need to tell it here. Why did Charlie remain in the classroom all those years? He was always popular with his students. His degrees are impressive and the faculty likes him. Yet he was passed over for Department Chair when he told the truth about the school at an interview. The questions were progressing along with smiles on all sides of the long table when one stone-faced woman interrupted, "What's the tardy policy at Royal Oak?"

"Next semester we're going to have one," Charlie replied and no amount of explanation helped him then. A sensible person would have used different words. They thought he was a smart-ass or, at the least, telling stories out of school!

My husband, like the other teachers, takes the spring and winter holidays; so we plant tomatoes or watch the snow fall, depending on the season. Pulling weeds all summer helps me too. I think Charlie likes the planning, the color in the Burpee Seed Catalog, its glossy pages. An oasis in our own back yard. A school vacation with Melody had a whole new set of frustrations and often the public watching us—with sympathy. Change doesn't help. It scares her. Ralph Waldo Emerson had a dim view of travel. "Though we travel the world over to find the beautiful, we must carry it with us or we find it not." As you can see, I try to console myself with literature as much as my husband does. We are both English majors, after all. I just couldn't abide teenagers. Their turmoil and rage seemed too much for me. I made a fast change, immersed myself in elementary education, and took an immediate Masters. Kindergarten, on the other hand, cheers me and I made my room one big collage with corners of comfort for the kids, a rocker for me and a desk I brought in myself—big and old and painted navy blue. A few cheap chairs too. Wrapping their seats in corduroy takes little more than pushing flat thumbtacks in a board. Why do you think upholstery is listed in jobs for the retarded? I liked to stay in the classroom or breathe the air on the playground. I usually stood back of the merry-go-round in the late afternoon sun with Band-Aids in my pocket and no thought of home.

My room was mine all day. I had yearned for the simple and clear cut and there I found it, long past quitting time. High school, on the other hand, is fragmented. Passing from class to class and sharing a desk was not for me. Once I had to tell a boy, a precocious speller: "Now let's get a few things straight. You can't print FUK on your papers or bite your teacher." He didn't last long. His parents moved away after their first conference. They had seen too many programs for the emotionally disturbed in the Midwest and that was where the boy was headed. They knew it before I showed them the papers. He was an exception. Most children here are in good shape and they loved what they found in my room. It helps a lot to work for a principal you admire in a school you can be proud of.

After Melody's asleep, Charlie and I read in wing chairs that cry out for new upholstery. We share a footstool. We are truly absorbed. "Away" my husband calls it. Un-American as it is, this room has no speakers or TV in front of us. We keep an old twelve inch black and white in the kitchen for the morning news and I have to hit it hard to make it work. A task I bend to with some grace. *The New York Times* comes in a blue plastic bag and hits the front door around 6:00 AM. I'm awake then, thinking. Sleep comes easier to Charlie.

My name is Elizabeth and I've been called everything from Liz to Beth but would choose Betty if a choice were to be had. Mrs. Anderson is what my students say, and my name is easy for them to remember. Not always so for my colleagues. Detroit is an ethnic community and from football players to GM executives, long names that end in "ski" that take practice to pronounce and spell are the norm: Medowitz, Rutkowski, Niedowitz, Koltonovitz, the possibilities are endless. Polish jokes have gained a foothold here, but I never laugh. That's another story, for racism in Detroit leaks on everything; and there's a dirty name for everyone and three for the Italians; and yes, such hate boils up every 20 years or so aiming to destroy the city. The last riot came in 1967. But we are a tough lot. Even the guilty ones like us who pay top dollar to live in this beautiful enclave with sidewalks and Tudor architecture between the mile roads, and within spitting distance of the zoo where anyone can hear the fountains splash and watch those giant turtles inch forward, protected from the heat and us by their shells and a low lying fence.

We're planted firmly in this tiny suburb, the three of us, and have no aspirations for a group home or independent living for her; both choices chuck full of the old abuses the vulnerable have always endured. Independent living, though touted and pushed, is really a new kind of slavery designed to save the state money. The Chinese say that the first step to wisdom is to call things by their proper names. In Special Education you can get so far away from those names you feel you are at the bottom of a well where darkness feels like death itself.

You know those nightmares. Everyone has a pet dream that won't stop. Well, mine was the night the electricity went off and the clocks stopped. When I went to wake up Melody for school, she had already left the house barefoot—carrying her shoes out to the minibus while she walked on through the season's first snowfall. There may have been no noise from her alarm clock, but she found her clothes set out the night before and her sack lunch. Her bus driver reported me for neglect, but that was years ago and actions speak louder than my sorry explanations. It never happened again. All the other bus drivers were nice and they dealt with those heavy wheelchairs and perseveration twice a day in heavy traffic. They faced reality first thing every morning—five days a week.

One year, Melody and I bought her new driver a cashmere scarf at T.J. Maxx, brown to match her car coat, and I like to think the driver actually feels our gratitude against her face when she wears it. We put the scarf in one of those sacks that have replaced boxes and wrapping paper; the driver teared up when she reached inside. I could have given her a bottle of Crown Royal, but that wouldn't sit well with the Board of Education and we both had too much to lose by breaking the rules. "Merry Christmas," she said with her fast Spanish accent, content with what she got. For that moment, I felt Melody was safe, yet I know no one is—least of all her. "I know none of us is protected. We just have to go on," I learned that from Paul Newman in *The Verdict*, Charlie's favorite movie.

So we left each morning, the children first and then my husband and I. He would drop me off at the entrance to the elementary school early on winter mornings and I walked home at 4:00. We hired a woman to be there when Melody's key turned in the lock. It was a deal for both of us: two hours at $8 an hour. She let

Melody count out the cookies, and she always had cocoa in two mugs, ready. They'd eat the snack in the kitchen and then set the table for dinner. Melody folds the silverware in napkins at home too, and the woman added plates and bowls. Our other children are at the far edges of that memory. I could smell the contents of the crock pot when I walked into the vestibule. Our bread came sliced thick. We'd peel fruit for dessert weekdays. My husband still brings home a sponge cake on Friday night, but sweets are not our nightly fare. Usually, I keep a square candle in the middle of the table and he lights it. We eat on place mats. I keep them in all the primary colors, a carryover from childhood when "reinforce" was our password. Melody loves them. She chose those same colors for her bathroom in stripes. In many ways, her pleasures became ours.

During dinner we'd watch that show about a Detroit carpenter—the reruns too—and it was a comfort to all of us. We were never bored. Sometimes we would say the lines along with the actor. I soon stopped aching for new experiences or dinner table conversations like the Kennedy's were rumored to enjoy. I have a hard time believing all that crap anyway. Current events? Political debates? Games to sharpen the mind? It's a long way from the Kennedy dinner table to "Home Improvement." I have accepted what we have now, though I'm afraid to name it.

Dinner was crazy when the older kids lived at home. I want to forget that I expected too much from them and what it feels like to know Isobel didn't move to Japan to learn the language and explore the literature; and Alaska has about as much appeal as an empty vinegar bottle to John. He always hated shoveling snow and ice skating in zero temperatures. But Alaska is a long way from us;

a deal, he says, and the land is cheap. Jenny Grier is still in graduate school at Wayne State. She's collected three degrees, lives in a boarding house, and has paid for it all herself. She worked at The Pontchartrain Wine Cellars until it closed. Now she's a cocktail waitress somewhere. Restaurants come and go; I can't keep track of her.

Our days seem predictable now; the answering machine keeps out salesmen and telemarketers. We are together, mindful of a tomorrow that might not be so peaceful. What comes next is a mystery, not just for us, but for the whole country. September 11th was just another morning at first, and now we know way more than we could have imagined about hate. At night, my husband's arms or back, depending on our mood, made all the difference. There's a shortage of jazz stations in Detroit, so we'd drift to the sounds from our own CDs. For a long while Coleman Hawkins was our favorite. We didn't have to talk to feel connected, as our days passed and accumulated into a week.

At my school, I lived a different life. I was in charge in my room and on the playground. Yet I dozed during those deadly teachers meetings full of jargon and pretense. I didn't snore or slip off my chair, so nobody noticed. They had problems of their own, my colleagues. Never enough money and divorce was rampant. "Nest-egg" was no longer a word used in a teacher's lounge. The lucky ones taught summer school. Each day ended with a hot bath if I was in the mood. I counted on those sign posts the way some people treasure their safety deposit boxes.

I have always avoided anything mechanical, technical. Charlie takes care of all that. My mother loved cars and could fix one. Our car was old and needed a lot of fixing but it was never fixed. She could also add long lists of numbers in her head; a skill left over from her job as a cashier at C.F. Smith's Grocery. She grew up in Pleasant Ridge and her father managed a store in nearby Ferndale.

Whatever she liked, I resisted; so even now in an age of powder puff mechanics and highly touted independence, I not only do not read my car manual carefully, I kick the washing machine when it jams. So it was with deep misgivings that I accepted a laptop from Charlie last Christmas and thus surrendered to email and the Internet.

All along, however, I resisted the cell phone and was fond of citing statistics of auto wrecks where they had played a part. I had some sympathy for loud mouths who gave orders to a secretary who may or may not have existed—puffing up their image to match the bloat in their stomachs, not to mention those invisible phones that made me think that the women behind me in the grocery lines were either talking to themselves or me. But, finally, our family became connected because of Melody; and our phones, identical, all have little circles with our initials so we won't get confused.

Retirement. My school books are in the basement. Still in boxes. And my painted furniture that needs repainting is there too. What did I expect? I now have quiet afternoons and long nights to think about this question; and so far, my thoughts are fragmented. Scraps of sentences. Imagery that surfaces, then fades as the hands of our bedroom clock circle its center. It is a clock Charlie made in his evening pottery class. The hands were ordered from a catalogue and I remember the day a nail went in the wall to hold it. Will the nail hold? Or will the clock crash down in the middle of the night when the March wind enters through an open window? I think about these possibilities since I have been confined to this four poster bed with its down pillows and soft summer blanket. My eyes move from the clock to the family photographs and back again.

W. Somerset Maugham saw bed rest in the best possible light. His bed being a retreat piled with books across from open windows. No deadlines or visitors. His meals appeared as regularly as the afternoon sun shone, and the maid closed the curtains after she set the tray in front of him. Maugham and I approach this thing as the elderly approach life after high expectations, sudden shifts, and the brick wall of reality. Or do we? I have the flu and there is no maid here.

CHAPTER 4

When I'm alone, away, and take a few days to breathe (a luxury supplied by my husband's largesse and love), I change temporarily and can honestly say that I sleep better, think more, and my only goal each day is not just relief. A weekend with a girlfriend, to laugh, or sit and tell the truth.

But now that we are retired and thrown back on ourselves, without the certainty of the school day or the safety of the bus, my husband and I are fearful. We worry about supported employment, cutbacks, job coaches, the unwatched moment. Our own deaths. There is no trust fund yet, but we own our house and car, and our drawers are chock full of insurance policies. So far, nobody has offered to take charge of Melody. And knowing there are no answers—just endurance, restraint, and the relief and lure of black comedy—the two of us gradually found solace in small and ordinary things, a garden of six rows, a thick bank of butterfly bushes on one side of the house, and a full overgrown hedge on the other. Our honeysuckle is as thick and certain as a fat woman's expanding body—twined along the back fence. Our rows of vegetables could be mistaken for flower-beds, for the earth holds dark and light green lettuce and the best tomatoes we can find, staked!

Parsnips lie hidden below the ground and even raspberries—not so easy to cultivate because mowing our lawn requires some rearranging of their branches. It's a salad garden and the source for a Christmas recipe with clotted cream—the parsnips, that is.

    I don't cook on Thanksgiving. Charlie sets the alarm to stuff the turkey and Jenny Grier comes home with her pals, and sometimes my best friend flies in from out of town, older and thinner in a wool dress. I like to watch her in a chair with her legs crossed. My foot shakes in the same position, so I wear flannel pants with a belt that set me back some cash—a designer thing that caught my eye in Marshall Fields on a snowy day last January when I wanted some hot buttered rum and had nowhere to go. As for blouses, mine are all white and come from a used clothing store in Ferndale. I told you, simplicity appeals to me now as it always has; but when my leg continues shaking and my head feels ready to explode before the squash casserole arrives, it's hard to make choices. White blouses help then. Anyway, everybody brings a dish. My contribution is a jar of mint jelly and a clean house; our version of a Norman Rockwell meal when once steaming bowls, all prepared by the mother, took their places on the table! I sleep late on Thanksgiving while Melody watches Charlie baste the turkey. She laughs when he pulls the neck out of the carcass and helps him by separating the liver and heart from its little gauze bag. What the hell does free range mean? A high price and an escape from the freezer for the doomed bird. "How far can they roam? And who is really free?" Last year, a cynical mother said this to me at a sex education meeting right before the holidays, as we waited for our girls to emerge from talking to a nurse and football player whose charity work with the retarded earned them citations from the city. "Your daughter knows all the right words," they said in unison, packing up the two anatomically correct dolls with moveable parts. Then we drove home in the other mother's van. I have no pride about accepting a free ride.

It was a small sex education class and minuscule attendance at the demonstration part. Most parents like to pretend sex doesn't exist and say they have already informed their retarded children at home—another lie, I'll bet. I stretch the truth too, though, sometimes: "Listen, Melody, you only make love after you have a job with benefits." My husband laughs, but he waits to laugh till later when the curtains blow across the windowsill and somehow moonlight slips past us. Yes, I cry, he laughs, and there is softness to both sounds. To be honest, almost every retarded grown-up ends up being abused in some way, mostly sexual, all in due time; and it should come as no surprise, the shrink told me matter-of-factly, that all those jokes about the ideal wife (a retarded girl whose parents own a liquor store) that don't bear repeating and the textbook percentages, I forget the percentages in them, but I slammed the book shut when I first read how and why and when, two facts were clear: being pretty is no asset and it's illegal now to sterilize anyone—at least in Michigan.

So-called progress continues and soon we can kiss abortion good-bye too if we endure another go round with the far right. Why am I concerned? A grandmother with <u>two</u> retarded offspring, please! Don't get me started on politics. Socialism makes the most sense to me. But no socialists ran in the last election. Now that these CEO's have been exposed for what they always were—greedy and full of every clichéd rationalization invented, socialism makes even more sense. Enron. Haliburton. I'm a registered Democrat and I vote every primary, every election. Things have come to a sorry pass for me to be proud of what should be expected of everyone, because the dwindling number of votes continues downward with each passing year.

Melody votes, though. All of this hard won normalcy is supposed to be an enormous improvement over the ignorance of the fifties. Just as there are sex education classes after school, someone demonstrates voting machines in a special class on Saturday. And after weeks of practice and praise, the afflicted walk up to the grade school tables, write their names in cursive slowly, and piss off those in the line who don't see their faces of total concentration. There are no machines. At such times I keep my mouth shut.

When did I eventually cancel *The New York Times* and stop checking out CNN? I kept a book close by so it wasn't reading I gave up, just daily news print. And I only saw movies on cable; neither crowds at Blockbusters nor the lines at the theaters seemed worth it. I fill my need for drama by never missing *Homicide, Life on the Street, The Sopranos,* and now *101 Center Street*. The years pass with this terse dialogue and actors so fine, they take your breath away.

Alan Arkin is my favorite actor and directors like Barry Levinson and Sidney Lumet know the score too; be it in Baltimore or New York, their sounds ring true. I watch reruns too, but Charlie draws the line there. He has a wood shop with a big clock, a heater, and a poster of James Dean smoking a cigarette on what looks like a pew lifted from an old church. I think there's an American flag in the background of the poster. Our son, the one in Alaska with an acre of ground and no wife, put it up there; and it is still attached to the door—even though the edges of the cardboard are not what they once were. Neither am I what I once was. And that's what I see clearly and what scares me most. I'm not talking about the ordinary loss of innocence that age brings. I'm talking about what races through my head when I'm not lost in a book or movie, when I'm not folding sheets for Melody's bed, or watching Charlie make bird houses for Habitat for Humanity. When all these merciful distractions have vanished.

CHAPTER 5

There were two moments in my life very much alike; the night I attended my first Recreation Therapy Dance at Pontiac State Hospital. Church workers manned the refreshment table, and former patients came as sure-fire dance partners for the insane. I was a volunteer, a do-gooder, and what I saw there hit me up close. I wasn't prepared for the state dresses, Dutch Bobs, and glazed eyes—so many all at once. I never went back. Then, the afternoon I saw the Christmas Program at Melody's Special Ed Pre-School where mothers brought enough cake to serve a wedding party, thin napkins from McDonald's, (the red and green ones had been mislaid because mothers like us keep losing stuff), and a huge coffee pot with decaf, hot, but weak. God forbid we should get jacked up, more nervous than we already are.

    A sibling floated the napkins over the audience as the mothers concentrated on their retarded elves being led around the stage while the oldest ones banged on a xylophone. There was a full group, but the flute and drum stayed frozen watching the napkins drift through the air. Melody tried to sing, but she is tone deaf and her voice dwindled from the pitch of a cheerleader to a silent O and she looked straight at me. Dovie was the mother with no teeth who couldn't get a handle on napkin boy. It's called familial retardation, and I had never thought about it before. I'd taken a day off work for this event, booked a ride with a dentist's wife in designer jeans and a single gold chain. After stuffing ourselves with cake and tap water, we rode home. "Thanks," I said. The dentist's wife nodded. The sound of the car door slamming came next.

Eventually, Melody returned with the car pool and spent all her time before dinner trying to get the song to her satisfaction. I sent out for Chinese and opened a bottle of port. Right away, I saw what danger loomed ahead and soon became just a former customer at Sam's liquor store. "Port?" said Charlie. No, Port goes with walnuts at Christmas, and Christmas was coming. I would wait. I wondered how I would steady my feet at our annual tree trim party, but I did. I talked non-stop and stayed away from the punch bowl. An hour before midnight, I took two sleeping pills and we left the mess for morning. My husband, Charlie, has never been much of a drinker and he didn't see the elves anyway. He has his own anguish and that's a story in itself, not a digression.

"Get a job away from children," a social worker said.

"You're making a big mistake, kids all day long and Melody at night. What do you really want, collapse or sex?"

She had a way of laying it out too soon. I walked out. Let her figure out the answer. I paid her bill, but not before she sent it to collection and Charlie raised the roof!

"You'll ruin our credit rating," he yelled. I walked out on him, too. But I continued teaching school.

CHAPTER 6

I've hated clichés since I first found out what one was. So why have I latched on to this one? *Work with what you have.* Well, I have more energy and more time to think now that everyone's gone away but Melody; and Charlie and I are here alone with the long afternoons. It took months for me to calm down after all the hoopla of retirement. In the beginning we stayed close to *Law and Order* reruns; they begin at 1:00PM, reappear at 7:00PM, and slow down at 11:00PM, so you can see just how much worry they could blot out, at first, for us both. Then I stopped the repeats, until I finally was shamed into cutting down to one. Now we are actually working together with the TV off.

We've read biographies and novels, side by side, and split the dinner work; him cleaning up and me arranging a meal on Melody's neat background of primary colors. She made our place mats—woven, they are. But those bits of cooperation between Charlie and me aren't close to really working together. As teachers and parents, we are used to bossing others around and so we have guarded against it with each other—or we would never have come this far. We have to boss Melody much of the time, check, wait, ignore. It's a matter of verbs.

I'm talking about mutual decisions about something outside Melody's life—like could the dining room be painted navy blue when the library remains pale gray? It was easy to agree on the library because the books provided all the color the room would take, but a navy blue dining room took some persuasion and concessions. Way more than usual. Why? Charlie got to choose the bathrooms, (he's still screwing around with paint samples), so I had to make it navy blue myself. I couldn't accept white woodwork. The color had to hit the ground and the floors sanded just so, even though we tacked on the cost of a motel with adjoining rooms while a crew came in with their brushes and cans. The man in charge of the work crew was from Israel—honest and fast and friendly. One worker was from Peru and another from Mexico City, the hills behind Mexico City actually. He told us his life story and the story of the man from Peru and we ordered pizzas every day and popped coke cans in the afternoons. It's easy to work when you're not alone.

Then I recovered all of the director chairs and sofa in the same tweed—a blue with red specks—and bought new lampshades—all alike, though one is bigger. We took down the chandelier since we use those block candles anyway and, of course kept Melody's pile of place mats. We bought new slippers, instead of a rug or carpet because Melody still hasn't stopped nagging for a dog and I'll never be able to endure the smell of piss locked in a carpet, if I give in. I have some dog lover friends who try to convince me that I have my priorities skewed when I enter their front doors with a spray bottle of Chanel No.5; but they're nuts, not me. "Why ask for more trouble?" I say. In fact, I say it far too often because Charley is a soft touch.

Our dining room table has leaves enough to seat ten, so we stored them just in case we ever feel up for a party or somebody gets married. "What about Jenny Grier?" Charlie doesn't give up hope. "Jenny's done well to be working at all. It's always a recession in Detroit!"

Jenny Grier is Charlie's favorite, the true intellectual among us. She followed in the family tradition, and her MA in Art History makes her sought out at openings and parties, some parties—but now she seems to think that a foreign language is going to help so she's taking Spanish classes and just came back from a month in Costa Rica, immersed. She's found work on Woodward Avenue six blocks from her boarding house. If anyone asks me, I say she works for the FBI, the food and beverage industry, so people with sense don't ask me any more questions.

So here we are with the third coat about to go on the library walls. I thought we had curtains to worry about too. When, all of a sudden, I thought, "Why bother?" The dining room faces the backyard and it's already enclosed, isn't it?

Charlie swears he can build a partner's desk out of a slab of countertop and hold it up on each end with a filing cabinet and I believe him. We both take this decorating too seriously—afraid of what follows after the last recovered cushion is in place. He hasn't told me what color he's picked for the countertop, but he'll have no quarrel with me. After awhile, I give up easy. What difference does it make now? It wasn't always this way. We've had Saturdays when the whole family left the house, taking Melody with us, while we battled over how cheap the porch furniture should be and I said it was crazy to buy Adirondack chairs, no matter how durable. Every choice mattered then.

"Who do you think you are, an East Coast Preppie?" I would scream.

"Shut up!" Charlie talked loud enough to scare me, and then we fell in each other's arms, knowing we were upset about Melody's new teacher who would have made a fine used car salesman, so adept was she at a manufactured grin and a load of crap so deep we needed fishing waders to get through it. I'd stopped kicking the lights on by then, when I broke a toe, and now I know why. Psychiatry has its place and the price is cheap, considering. It took about a year of trial and error to find a good one, the red-faced doctor who recommended vacations.

"You'll have to do something with your hostility—or it will eat you alive," he said.

More than one person had the nerve to tell me that. And I knew it was true. Though I crossed them off my list the same day they said it. The doctor I couldn't cross off. He was the only one who could take my rage and give me back even harder truths to consider.

Where do we go from here? I thought, once Charlie and I were getting along again. You can't decorate forever. I wanted a new look for me too. I couldn't make up my mind, so I took out a *Land's End* catalogue and ordered pink and gray cord overalls—a pair each and thought about what I could buy to last until I die, feeling especially old that morning. I added six white turtlenecks. I have white hair and thick ankles, and I hated those old ladies in the movies, you know, the Greek ones at the side of the road in 1940 black and white films, crones all in black; almost as much as I hated the blue rinsed set, in Birmingham and Bloomfield Hills, in navy silk as if all the joy had been taken from their lives and ready-made funeral attire would fill the spaces as they walked up the main drag pretending to window shop. Searching for something to fill their empty lives after their morning golf games.

For now, these overalls will do and for summer we have enough leftover tee shirts to go into business. Here with Charlie in the library, plastic taped to the floor, and a pompous voice on NPR announcing the composers as if the DJ owned them, I feel peace. I can ignore her confidence, for that's what I'm envious of. I can watch Charlie's roller begin in a corner and cover all the old smudges and mistakes and pushpin holes. He had spent a week patching and sanding before he took out the roller. And now sitting here watching him work is the high point of my day.

He's not painting the outside of our house; those high ladders have their own risks, so we both observe the power washing crew. Even if the men come late, they are done before noon and the result, pure white, is consolation enough for me. There's smog in most cities now. Chicago is still brown, the air, that is. But somebody told me Newark has cleaned up its air. I'm the type who must see to believe. All these lies about Melody's fate have soured me. It's as if I held a measuring stick in my hand now and use it to tell just how far from the truth things really are.

We're not going to make a career out of travel, like other retired teachers. We both agree on that. We rip up the tour brochures, the AARP issues, even letters from teachers we once trusted. When September 11th came and went, that tape of the towers and the plane spun in my head for weeks without the music they added for TV, and I felt sure I'd never reach higher than the roof of a greyhound bus or feel safe outside a roomette on Amtrak. I called for pamphlets about deals for the bus and the railroad and then filed them away. $37 for airfare from San Antonio to New York, my cousin told me! Her daughter lives there and she couldn't resist. Finally, I wondered whatever made me think I was safe in the first place! I got over it and flew, ordering bottled water and sucking in the stale airplane air while the little pillow and navy blanket were loaned to me and the light above my head clicked off. Safety is a joke. I'd known that all along.

CHAPTER 7

My best friend found the school, old, and New England's best. Batesville required a large preppie wardrobe; and, let me say right off, it's no accident that the New York State prisons, asylums, and schools for the afflicted are tucked behind and beside some of the most beautiful lakes and mountain resorts, and the richest little towns I've ever seen up close. Batesville is tucked a little farther away, near wine country. Therefore, safety inside the school grounds was nothing I questioned. One fact is clear, but it was buried then. Employees come and go and nothing is really predictable. Just like the school bus driver in North Dakota who took his charges on a sudden all-day bus ride with plenty of food on board and finally turned himself in to a cop in a mall parking lot. Fear is a fact and it ain't goin' away. And I am afraid; as afraid as those waiting mothers who trusted the bus driver.

"He loved his job," said a neighbor, "Proud of his students, and his background checked out."

Well, Melody was assaulted at Batesville. Who did it? Who knows? How do you interview the retarded? How do you interview anyone when you find out months later what really happened from the shrink who said that the specific content of her delusion can't be imagination. Melody, mercifully, I like to think, had a psychotic break that day before the New England sun went down. Thought she ate her roommate with a fork for supper.

You can't get away from the percentages, and if you think job screenings there, or anywhere else, are foolproof, you are a ninny—one of those old-fashioned words that hits the modern mark.

"Why didn't you sue?" one of my so-called friends said.

"Nothing like a retarded, crazy person for a witness, eh?"

Americans are taught to sue if the frozen custard gives them freezer burn. Christ! I had perfected swearing into an art form. And, in those days I envied anyone who believed in Christ until the day another mother told me that stuffed celery was one contribution too many to the PTSA.

"Don't you know Jesus is going to come back and make all these children right again? You're working too hard, Elizabeth, and I can't bake another cake anyway, I'm having my Bible study class for coffee."

"It's Labor Day," I said, "Where will your son go?"

"He'll be upstairs. He likes his room."

Her husband left the two of them after kindergarten. "Five years of this is my limit," he said, so the woman turned to her pastor. Is this where a belief in Jesus takes you? I stepped back. We were at one of those support groups funded by leftover Federal money, the kind that is now a thing of the past. I heard a woman with a ten-year old, pregnant again, after her ultra sound made a second Fragile-X child close to real. She was eight months pregnant, in fact.

"I don't believe in abortion," she smiled in the Laura Ashley dress she had bought too big and remodeled. A talented woman with patterns, size 4.

"There's a reason for everything." She had a breathy voice.

"Do you mean a plan?" I said.

She turned away and shared her recipe for meatballs with an eager first timer. At least she's not a vegetarian, I thought, pouring a second cup of coffee and spilling it on myself. I needed to go to the toilet, and when I was there, safe, I sobbed inaudibly. Then, I went for help.

Coming out of the bathroom, I passed the new mother with the sleeping infant and meatball recipe and drove straight to a Clinique counter.

"In the old days, you called it Erase," I smiled at the clerk, "And I bought it by the pound."

"Well, now they call it Concealer and it comes in a tube. Do you have a charge account with us?"

She must have noticed how disheveled I looked, clutching my books and overstuffed purse. I pushed my credit card across the counter and bought two tubes. You need cover-ups to keep on going. Going where? A question I keep asking myself. I should have asked it for the whole family, not just me and Melody.

CHAPTER 8

There is more about boarding school that I haven't told you. I had to bring Melody home. It was an ordinary plane and the flight attendants were no better or worse than usual; so I knew a fast strategy was imperative. After we were in the sky and the cart was juiced up, I walked to the back near the toilets.

"I have a retarded crazy girl with me who has had a load of Thorazine; I have more in my pocket, and more in my husband's hand when we reach the gate. So if you help us, I think we'll make it. I want you to think back to the fifties when customers, especially those with babies, were offered every courtesy from warmed bottles to soft words, captain's wings, coloring books and anything else you can think of—extra cokes. Hopefully, she'll sleep after all those courtesies and the medicines."

"I'm her mother and I love her. Something unexpected and terrible and unknown happened to her at her boarding school and she's going straight to the safety of a hospital when we reach the ground. Her father faces most everything, but he couldn't face this." Then I touched the flight attendant's hand and walked back to my seat.

"I'll take bottled water," I said when I was asked and my daughter said, "May I have two packs of cookies, please?" Manners are copied. Manners are a comfort when you are scared mindless. The flight attendant said, "For you, dear, we have hot chocolate, too. It comes in packets." I cried, but nobody noticed.

In the evenings, after our daily visit to Melody's ward at Havenwyck, we ate supper out, close to the hospital. There wasn't much to say. What we wanted to ask, we seemed to forget, like leaving my glasses in the kitchen when I take the newspaper back to the bedroom to make sure there are still problems worse than mine, that the president hasn't been maimed, that the crime rate has steadied itself.

Our conversations were like that, misplaced, while silence hung in the air and if the dishes crashed or the spoons rattled, I never noticed. The past ran a race in my head in the kind of circle that jolts as it spins. One thing we counted on as we left the hospital was dessert. From smushed apple pie to double scoops of ice cream, we ordered and ate fast. My husband, who usually orders decaf, took regular and I knew why. Sleeping now was a dream in itself, and many nights we would both wake up wet and frightened. Melody was in the hospital for three months.

I did wasteful things then. I sent a $50 bowl of roses to the policeman who treated us like human beings while the showboat psychiatrist who couldn't keep his face off TV admitted Melody. She followed him, docile, smiling:

"I ate my roommate for dinner with a big fork. How can I find her?"

I had to call the station house to get his extension, and then I asked myself why I had to ask for it. How many Prince Reddings work out of the Hancock Station?

Finally, after four-point restraints had bloodied her legs and every medicine tried, a miracle happened. The doctor had a friend at Receiving Hospital who was experimenting with a new drug already popular in Europe, Clozaril. Strings were pulled and Melody became part of the study. She was sane in a week, discharged two days later. Don't tell me you don't believe in medicine. You have to need it to get the point of it. You have to almost reclaim your rosary to know the score. But I didn't. We just took her home and went right on. Public School is there for all. Prep School had been a big mistake. We gave up thinking about our marriage. We forgot romance. With Clozaril, she didn't hear voices or want to help a little girl crying in distress on Woodward Avenue at 3:00 AM. We slept and stopped expecting what others had. And I clutched that researcher's hand so tight he had to shake it out, but he smiled at me. The bill was $70,000 because the insurance ran out. We took out another loan and were glad to pay it off. Living with a crazy person is beyond my strength and anything was better than that. Charlie agreed.

CHAPTER 9

"I have a quote for you," said my husband one night after Melody had fallen asleep and we were too tired to stop her CD player. I'm not fond of "The Yellow Submarine," but I don't hate it either; I was just tired of the Beatles. My feet were shoeless and embedded in the living room footstool by the time the song had begun again. "What quote?" I said, looking into his eyes and beyond. Then we both realized he'd forgotten the bloody quote. Our memories are not what they once were.

We walked into the kitchen for a late supper. Snow lay in drifts outside the window. "Steak?" he asked. I can't argue with him. If he had pushed it, I'd have had an 8-ounce steak, all things being equal; but I don't eat much beef anymore after a gallery owner I know contracted Mad Cow. "Two lamb chops will do nicely," I say, exercising some restraint, "And you can double up on the spinach." It happens to be my favorite. As he cooks, I put out the plates and think about mealtimes when the children voiced their objections to vegetables and teased each other. John Baxter had a list of numbered off-color jokes and they would demurely trade-off the numbers and laugh like banshees when the girls protested. Ours was a noisy house, but I never minded that. A blizzard once kept us safe inside and I spent the day simmering chicken soup and skimming off the fat. Jenny Grier made dumplings and we watched that thriller with Barbara Stanwyck confined to bed, *Sorry Wrong Number*, with her husband plotting her demise. John Baxter was always home too with an airplane model, absorbed. Snow days, the school system called them. We'd play "Old Maid" so Melody could be part of it all. We'd pretend we were challenged by puzzles for five-year olds. It was fun. Fun for me and Melody, for my other children must have been great actors, so full of guilt and pity were they. I was a fool, but I didn't know it then!

CHAPTER 10

"What is a friend?" I often thought, and my friend at the time always had an answer for me. She listened to my speeded-up recommendations for novels that she had to read for a few true accounts of lives like ours. I usually called when she was fixing dinner, but she never asked me to call back later. She ordered the books and read them. So for me our lunches were bliss. Just chicken salad, a medicinal Chablis, and serious talk. My friend was solid and honest and she had time to digest those books. She volunteered four days a week and it took her away to soup kitchens and what used to be called Victory Gardens downtown, where the weeds were waiting to be pulled and you could touch collard greens and zucchini up close, and see fires burning in barrels after the September harvest when some men carried cell phones and others wore the kind of gloves they used to sell at the hardware stores when I was growing up in Troy. Whole streets had been leveled by the '67 riots and planting vegetables in that dirt seemed like saying they and we might endure. The city itself was another story.

Her path to survival was different, yet we fit together. My friend ran. Gradually at first. Then for an hour on week days, and finally marathons. Her medals, and they accumulated, hung along her basement stairs where Ball jars sat in rows. Her washer was in the kitchen so not many people saw her medals, but I did and they encouraged me. I loved to touch them. I'm the most sedentary creature alive, but I soon started walking on the sidewalks with Melody on the weekends with no destination in mind, and my friend's image went with us. We were going nowhere, and no half-baked employment counselor could tell me different. Yet it felt good with Melody at my side. And I have to give the credit for this pleasure to my friend who ran marathons.

A job for Melody at the end of the line? By that time I was a cynic and so was her teacher who kept canceling work programs. No funds. Melody had always liked to tell him the plots of Walt Disney classics. "Maybe she can be a movie critic," her teacher winked. I didn't slap his pockmarked face, but I could have, and written him up but I was too tired to sit at the typewriter and there's only so much an IBM Selectric can do for you. Even with a white-out key.

"Let's go for a picnic," my husband said that night, so Saturday morning we drove Melody to Rouge Park with a sack lunch in her book bag. The picnic was an event. Charlie usually made Jenny Grier pancakes on Saturday and she didn't linger then like the rest of us or stick around to do the dishes. Jenny talked and paced and smiled at Melody and excused herself from the picnic. Home before dark though, and not a bother to anyone. I knew the pleasure of getting lost in a book, so I assumed that I understood her. I couldn't see what was clear to my friends. When I look back, Jenny Grier was lost even then, and earning another Master's degree is not going get her a better job. In some ways, she's grown farther away than the other two, though she's as close as twenty minutes in rush hour the way Charlie drives.

Isobel, the oldest, looks the best on the outside and if you didn't know her and know Japanese literature, you might not see her anguish. Taller than the rest of us with auburn hair, she is far from blending-in in Kyoto. She was a scholarship student from her first day in college to the moment her MA was in her hand. She was always part of that crowd that locks into the grindstone and stays on the fast track. She had worked summers for the FBI too, and saved her paycheck. She even bought a stripped down sewing machine and made everything she wore. Double duty dresses. Night gowns. She was never interested in fashion, only cover-ups; loose and swinging, in an era when people dressed like Madonna, that middle Michigan girl who spent a year at Ann Arbor before she left for New York. She sure knew what she wanted. Madonna embarrasses me, but I admire her drive.

I'm straying from the point. Isobel got her money's worth. Remnants from bedspreads and curtains and anything without sleeves were right up her alley. Her only vanity was shoes and she paid a fortune for the labels, Cole and Hahn, and she never failed to polish them. I thought I was getting close to her by reading all that Japanese lit in translation that Berkeley Medallion put out in the sixties, cheap. Mishima novels, (that was before he cut his guts out in public). Kawabata. The Nobel Prizes, the suicides, the beauty and sadness. I think she understood both, and Japan pulled her away from us.

She moved there to leave all that Melody represents. With a Master's in Comparative Literature in her hand, I guess she thought she'd specialize by osmosis; but I'm getting ahead of my story. She ran there to escape friends pulling back who would never let on how embarrassed they were in our house, and boys. She ran from boys and then men. Isobel, the bookworm with a locked-in family. There are lots of pretty girls out there who don't hide behind loose dresses, even if the dresses are black velvet at Christmas time. Her boyfriends lasted for six months tops, when she had them. "Guess who's not coming to dinner, Mom?" The reason went right over my head. I expected too much of myself and my children—all along. Way too much, and Charlie too, but at least he hasn't left yet. I know how lucky I am.

CHAPTER 11

All my life I thought about the big important things and waited. In the fifties, a girl was on her way to spinsterhood at 25. Some girls had shot gun weddings almost with their high school diplomas in their hands. Some had scholarships to college and went and stayed; others got cold feet during their senior year of high school and took a load of typing and stenography, and looked for a job downtown. A few lucky ones picked up a degree and an engagement ring, and slipped right into a June wedding, or August, if they waited too long to get on the church calendar. Grad school? Uncommon. Mostly men, already married; teaching assistants with wives who worked, or wives who didn't, with Irish twins. One girlfriend I had left town and was never heard from again. I pulled back as that news unfolded and I have never forgotten it.

I held out for a degree and a man who read books and didn't think the world stopped at the Ford Motor Company, someone who didn't get riled up over trivia. I didn't either in those days. So Charles and I married at the Shrine of the Little Flower; after all, both of us had been brought up Catholic and we had not yet fallen away. That would come later! I wore a cream silk suit because we had been closer than close for a year, and pure white still meant something. The reception was in my back yard and we stuck around until the sun went down and then loaded our gifts into a station wagon and drove away. After our honeymoon, we savored the best mattress sold by J.L. Hudson's—hard and guaranteed. The floors were varnished and the walls matched my wedding dress. We threw an Indian spread across the mattress and my mother made us curtains. One pull of a string and they were shut. It was a room full of sun and solitude, and our rent check was never late.

I loved sticking close to campus, walking to free concerts and lectures, and sitting in the snack bar at the Student Center. We stayed in that apartment for three years until the crib no longer held Isobel, whose room was a large coat closet. We took the door down and hung some of those tinselly looking things that went with the bed spread. We weren't much for parties at first—putting aside my entire check, all of it. "Paying rent is like tearing up twenty dollar bills," my mother said, "All you've got to show for yourself is a pile of receipts." So "Down Payment" became our slogan, and after work, we fell into each other's arms at 4:30.

I don't remember all we ate on weeknights, but some times it was Rice Krispies and bananas. Real teaching is exhausting. Sack lunches and milk in cartons—nothing complicated. I'm a slob if I don't watch myself, but I watched, and we used the two pewter plates, wedding gifts, and thick plastic glasses, so there wasn't much to break or clean up. The laundry was in the basement. I liked folding towels then when the towels were new and fluffy and warm, and you could dream about the future.

That was our first year—what we touched there in our studio apartment with its homemade mustard yellow bookcases lining one wall—the ones we painted in my father's front yard and then watched a horde of bees get stuck in. But that was the beginning, and now it's gone. So is teaching. I loved it so much that I still go over its ups and downs every day. What things shocked me the most, scared me the most, enraged me the most? The answers bubble up in time, but I know I miss the language of the youngsters, the Art Linkletter-type remarks. I miss being the bearer of heat and light and steadiness and color. I miss the magic of teaching what comes before reading.

I never realized how much teaching filled me up until now, when I have this chunk of freedom to worry through. The idea, I think, is to stay out of malls and grocery stores—Charlie and Melody actually like to stack the cans and count the apples. Melody knows most of the baggers from the special schools or recreation groups that she has been involved with over the years. Shopping is a social event for her.

She holds her father's hand in the Farmer Jack parking lot. They shop on Monday night at Kroger and on Thursday at the Farmer's Market. She bowls on Wednesday and we, like the rest of the bored world, see movies on Friday night, on cable. Monday night is "100 Center Street" and I follow the plot with Arkin's hopeless daughter and the hell he tried to play fair in. He's a judge and the show is riveting, like *Law and Order*. But you can't watch reruns forever; after a while, even Benjamin Stone and Jack McCoy seem like next door neighbors, too close.

I also watch *Judge Judy* every day at 4:00. Nowadays there's a judge sorting the liars out on some channel every afternoon. I want a reprieve, and Judge Judy is a sure thing. I set the table and cook supper during the commercials, but I'm sitting down and absorbed when her face reappears, glasses slipped a little, lips tight, mouth wide. She's in charge. Her voice loud, louder. Her words cut through everything: sorrow, belligerence, theft, and outrage. Be it roommates or parents or stepmothers, she thinks she knows who is wicked and who is blameless. Speed matters. Judge Judy is experienced, and most of the time she sees what is coming next—her verdict, if little else. I can't get enough of Judge Judy. There's a lot I want to forget. Even if it's only for 30 minutes. No fires, car wrecks, or murders, just the judge after forty years on the bench, in her lace collar and robe presiding and deciding.

Forget ordinary thoughts of death as one passes sixty—they're there, and there are plenty of them. What drives me wild is wondering what is going to happen when we're gone and all the evasions surrounding that fact stand out in neon! Who can we count on after the government provides what little it provides? And after the bank executor does whatever he does? Whose lives will be ruined? How far can anyone run?

Every Saturday I see an old woman and her handicapped son walking slowly, side by side, sometimes stumbling with plastic sacks in each hand, on the sidewalks near our house. I know they don't live nearby, but I have a fantasy that keeps me from cracking up the car as I pass them—that they live in Berkley and they walk through this neighborhood for its beauty and its sidewalks, not caring that it's the long way home. That someone will care for the son when his mother dies. That they will still have group homes then and old hotels won't swallow up this boy and others like him. That cruelty will be measured, and not come all at once and destroy what is left of his life. If I prayed, I'd pray for him. I'd pray for my daughter and myself. I'm in a bad place—disconnected and beyond. How else can I explain passing them by?

Then we had what seemed like a new problem, but it wasn't really—just the result of another one of Melody's mistakes, stepping out in front of a teenager covered with tattoos whose eyes didn't work right in the glare of the afternoon sun. A car crash. But that was 1997, and those five years are over. In 2002, when her knee ballooned, the surgeon said this time it would take six weeks, not a year, wooden crutches and soon a cane—not the long advance from a wheelchair to a new-fangled crutch that looked like a steel cage; a cage I forgot as soon as it was returned. The glistening steel, the sound of her leaning on that crutch as it tapped down the hall above the pool table in the re-done recreation room where her sisters and brother once played, argued, and dropped peanut shells all over the linoleum.

This time, Medicaid paid the bill and added an ice machine and three months of appointments with a physical therapist Melody fell in love with. His name was Connor and he was the only one in the big room with a heart and a white shirt to cover it. The others acted like exhausted robots waiting for the hands on the clock to find the number five. They all wore Swank watches and soiled blue jeans and talked to each other while their patients moved and stretched and waited. It just went on and on; but we, at least, had Mr. Connor.

Part of my problem was waiting far too long to say, "I can't stand it." My friend, no stranger to perseveration, could take it in the morning and after school too. But anybody's patience fails when there's no let up and a nine o'clock bedtime seems three days away. For retarded children, routine is the wire on which they hang the thin certainties of their days. Time is something many of them can't tell; so after the milk and cookies that follow the mini bus ride home, after washing up, and *The Brady Bunch*, it starts: "What happens next?"

There are suggestions: Call a friend, do one simple chore like putting out the clothes for the next day or pre-packing a lunch. "I'm bored." We were close to Woodward Avenue anyway, so I was left with inventing an errand—dental floss, a package of colored pencils. If my daughter could do a whole puzzle, I'd fill the living room with them. Spacial relationships and numbers are foggy for me too, but I can make change for a dollar and play a passable game of "Hearts." She can't. In fact, I really enjoy sticking a player with the Queen. It drains away some of my anger. But I don't need dental floss, and I am too much of a list-maker as it is.

Once I walked with Melody up the street in October. We were four blocks from a florist and took our time buying one red rose. Sometimes our goldfish would die, and we would head for Royal Oak to the pet store. That takes up a lot of time. But there is no end to the question, "What happens next?" until you feel you could slam an iron skillet down on a glass tabletop and scream,

"Not a God damn thing happens next!"

"Go take a bath."

"I don't care if you're not dirty."

Melody sobbed all the way up the stairs, let the hot water run cold and then pulled the bed covers over her head, terrified because I'm not usually a screamer, and she didn't know what to make of the sudden change. She fell asleep red-eyed, and I was left with a cold shower and a burnt roast. I've never been a gourmet cook and my husband knows, without a word, how hard it all is. Food is no disappointment to him. He eats lunches out at delis and sports bars, and he is at least away in a world where patience comes in different forms and minds are only clouded over temporarily.

On that particular night, the night I screamed, we decided to apply to the Eastern boarding school that my friend's daughter attended. It was the worst decision we ever made. A wardrobe of preppie clothes from Penny's, six pair of shoes from snow boots to flip-flops, tuition, and plane fare for six visits home—a $30,000.00 debt. We did it to save our marriage. Coming home for a quickie at noon was not my idea of romance. We thought privacy mattered then.

CHAPTER 12

Loquacious. Garrulous. Fancy words that applied to me and made my friends eventually disappear, all but one friend, and thus made Charlie's attention even more precious to me. After a typical day, Charlie and I sat, in the late hours between the children's bedtimes and ours, sharing the same footstool, with the Sears catalogue on the table and the Burpee Seed catalogue beside it. Back and forth to the kitchen with the teapot, I came. Reluctant to go to bed, Charlie having long since finished grading a pile of themes, folded now lengthwise with a rubber band around them. *Webster's Unabridged* closed tight on an end table. He listened to me then. As the years passed, words poured from my mouth overlapping into what the clinicians called an agitated depression. I couldn't shut up once I began. And no schoolmarm cover-up could hide my frantic monologue.

Once, I stopped talking. It was during Easter vacation, and I just left. I took my purse and a blazer and boarded a bus. In Detroit April can be cold. It was late in the afternoon and the bus was full of domestics coming home from work. I sat in the front just behind the driver. It was pretty quiet. You can be too tired to talk, and I certainly fit right in.

After we had traveled a few miles, a young boy got on and slowly counted out the fare. He was tall and wearing the sort of beanie with a propeller that we used to order with a cereal box-top and a quarter taped to cardboard. After depositing the coins, he looked around, and seeing an empty seat beside one of the ladies in the front row, he walked in that direction and before sitting down, he smiled. Then, in a halting, loud voice, he addressed the cleaning lady next to him: "Pardon me, ma'am, may I hold your hand?"

It was obvious, to me at least, that he was retarded. The cleaning lady could have said anything, but she turned to her comrades behind her seat and whispered, "I can't take this shit after working all day!" Nobody laughed. There were a few noises. Then quiet acceptance of whatever came along; but I never forgot that phrase. It summed up everything for me.

I don't know what I expected after that. One by one, the domestic workers left the bus, and the boy moved up near the driver until he, too, got off. I stayed in my seat until we got to Grand Boulevard, and then I took a transfer though I had no intention of going east or west. Instead, I started walking up Woodward Avenue and went all the way to the Detroit Public Library and then changed my direction and crossed the street where Rodin's *Thinker* stands in front of the Detroit Institute of Arts. All that white marble soothed me. The sun was still out, even if it was chilly, and I started to feel better.

Just the fact that those buildings were there and had been there when Charlie and I met, and had still been there when Isobel and Jenny Grier practically lived in them, and would be there after we were long gone. Maybe the library hours were shortened, maybe there was no longer a card catalogue, maybe the Patriot Act was making inroads on the freedom to read, but the marble steps and statues had lasted and would last. And, for a moment, that was enough. I got on the next bus and rode back home. Instead of boiling Easter eggs, I made chicken soup.

"Are you sick?" Charlie said, not knowing where I'd been, and I didn't tell him.

"No, just tired." I replied. He made supper that night.

CHAPTER 13

John Baxter was a cherished child, though I doubt if he ever felt like one. We had wanted a boy all along. Charlie, with all those stories about his three brothers, felt lost in a house full of women; and at last John arrived a week early. It was an easy delivery. Charlie built him a toolbox before my first labor pain, a heavy one with three holes in the handle for a screwdriver, hammer and wrench. And we bought those too, plastic, from Fisher Price. The girls played with them long before John could grasp a handle. In fact, Isobel hit me on the knee with the hammer when I was nursing him.

Things were a little chaotic, and when John was six months old, Melody was diagnosed. I had gone back to work by then, and John had graduated to a bottle. Rice cereal often covered him and his high chair because, though Charlie's aunt worked miracles with the kids, she ignored the messes. John was a good baby and gurgled his way through it all. After the news about Melody, the only time I relaxed was when I was feeding John in that old rocking chair we kept by the upstairs hall window.

Melody was in nursery school, and the teachers marveled at her big eyes and curly hair, but she had trouble learning the colors and following directions. She was a timid child. She copied what the others did. She tried. First we had her hearing tested. Then her eyes. The eye doctor said, "Nothing is wrong with her eyes, but if she were my daughter, I'd have her tested in the morning." The tests took a week.

Her scores were in the sixties across the board—Educable Mental Retardation, (EMR). We already knew the lingo. The lettering. The night we met with the psychologist we came home, put the papers on the end table, and cried so loud we woke John Baxter up. His crib was still in our room. "Don't kid yourself, Elizabeth—this is way worse than that fool psychologist wants you to believe." The psychologist had recommended after-school drills that he compared to dog training. Never go beyond point "A" until it is learned. Dog training! Instead, we enrolled her in a special program. P.S.-94142 wasn't very old then; and the government had created a program as close to ideal as we ever found. Her teacher came from Bryn Mawr.

John Baxter wasn't a good student. Distractible. A dreamer. Always polite, but his grades disappointed, and I guess it showed. He hid his report cards. Charlie spent whole evenings in the basement with John and we grew accustomed to the sound of saws and hammers. They built birdhouses, little blonde wooden cars with wheels of darker wood. Charlie even bought him one of those electric cars that run around the room on their own and the buzz of it drove me nuts. You'd think such efforts would all add up to something intimate.

John was quiet; a lot like Charlie came to be. A serious child. A worried teenager. He thought too much about the future. It's no surprise that he was taken in by cheap land in Alaska, and I can't help but think there is more to it than we'll ever know. When the day came that John realized he knew more than Melody, though she was almost four years older, he was stunned and kept trying to teach her subtraction with those little cards. Melody will never be able to make change for a quarter.

It was the rhythm of those summer mornings with John that I remember most vividly. Maybe the edges of those rhythms. The walks. John Baxter in his stroller, asleep or awake, when we passed the butcher shop, the post office. The girls were in day camp, and Charlie was teaching summer school. July was hot and the sidewalks were empty. Running, jogging had not reached its peak in those days, and besides, we were never out before ten. We ate lunch in the backyard and played with John and when he fell asleep, and we talked of Hemingway's Paris, Shakespeare & Company, Sylvia Beach and Gertrude Stein. We tossed words around and sometimes even read a Hemingway story aloud. Charlie taught a unit on Hemingway, and his sentences cut to the bone. We made up theme topics and stared at John Baxter's eyelashes. We adjourned to the screened porch if the rains came. It seemed nothing could spoil our lives.

Charlie usually came home with a stack of papers, folded lengthwise, and he might sort through five of them while I breast fed John. But that was later, after he picked up the girls, and they were down for their naps. His attention was on us, for the most part. The baby did the usual: gripped our fingers, peed in the air when his diaper was removed and sometimes hit us. We would laugh as we wiped our faces with one of his soft white diapers. Of course he cried too. In fact he had colic the first three months, but that was after supper. I never did figure out colic, and I consulted both Spock and Selma Fraiberg, who was still alive and teaching at the University of Michigan. They were her *Magic Years* and ours too!

We were lucky. Charlie's Aunt Ethel, a widow at 50, moved here from Chicago and worked five days a week during the school year; she never had a family. In those days it was risky to strain the male ego to learn why. Besides, who could afford fertility treatments if they even had them then? I don't know. Fertility was never my problem. Ethel lived in a flat in Ferndale and took the bus here every morning like clockwork. Ours was a perfect arrangement, and she went back to the Chicago relatives during her summers off. Charlie usually taught summer school, but I never did. Ethel worked for us for thirteen years and we gave her a small pension until she had a stroke. She never regained consciousness for a real good bye, but we sat with her for a week before they pulled the respirator. We took turns.

No matter what happens now, I have my memories of those mornings with John Baxter and afternoons with Charlie, the nearest thing to bliss I've had. Before reality hit us up close and changed everything. When I day dream, it's the past that drifts through my head. I've lost faith in the future.

CHAPTER 14

In the beginning, the year after Melody's diagnosis, I met a woman who drove out to the country weekdays while our children were in school, and stopped at little unlocked churches to pray for patience and ask, "Why?" She fell to her knees on a regular basis, hoping for help, for endurance. Her name was Mary Virginia and she never failed to cheer me up. Unlike that mother who thought Jesus would soon come to make everyone "right," my religious friend wasn't crazy. She was just a conventional woman with a pretty face and a willingness to laugh through the toughest spots. She had been a stewardess and she married well. A sense of humor seemed to help. Until one day, when she drove out to the gazebo on her aunt's property in Lake Orion and blew her brains out.

The funeral is not something I can talk about; but her daughter and my whole family were there. Her ex-husband lived on the West Coast, and he was impossible to reach in time for the service. The other mothers and what fathers were left in our so-called circle sent flowers and sympathy cards and covered dishes; but there was no wake and all that food just sat in my refrigerator because none of us could eat it. The day we got the news, Charlie and I held up until bedtime when we drank Crown Royal out of water glasses in our bedroom and finally fell asleep on top of the bedspread. Sometimes you can be too far gone to dream.

CHAPTER 15

Over the years I've watched and listened to other "special" mothers. I've made a lifelong friend with the marathon runner and traded practical information with many more women. I've even tried to help those who needed more than a smile or a lunch invitation, because it seemed heartless not to offer both. I still do it, but I'm careful to choose the restaurant and follow the meal with a dental appointment. If these appointments were all real I'd have worn away my teeth by now, or taken up with the dentist in his recliner. I have no problem with such white lies, and I pay for the lunches. Usually I just listen and offer Kleenex. The most I ever do is pass along some book titles and warning of restaurants to avoid where the "challenged" are not welcome.

But these gestures are not the point. Go to any Special Ed PTA or support group and you'll hear stuff that either breaks your heart or sets your teeth on edge. There is rarely an empty chair at these meetings. It's crazy but you're in it together, and you can't seem to stop. You eat stale cookies and ball up your napkin and try to concentrate on the speaker: wills, special trusts, birth control, guardianship.

I almost got lost in the details there. The point is anguish, an old fashioned word you don't hear enough of. It's as if you could deny its existence if you just leaned on Jesus Christ and all the babble that comes with him, and realized that your child is a gift who arrived as part of a master plan that will clarify itself after your life is over and someone in your family becomes guardian of what's left.

Ordinarily, these PTSA gatherings are mostly women, but not because the husbands are watching Monday midnight football or fooling around with your best friend. These "special" guys are gone; and they don't wait long to leave. The percentage for divorce in America hovers around 50% in these parts and rises to way beyond that when a damaged child appears in your arms. And two of them? I'll let you imagine the hopeless conversations, though there are some valiant tales of how people manage that horror show. All I can say is that I know how a couple felt who left their son in a wheelchair at the ER of some famous teaching hospital on the East Coast after their health failed and their money ran out. Like I said, other countries take a different view of misfits and the desperation that runs alongside them. We'll still be here talking to social workers not much smarter than their clients and eating our way through sleepless nights and the memoirs the library shelves hold, knowing no book can touch our own nightmares. I thought I'd heard it all:

"Nothing serious wrong with my kid—a little brain damage, but he'll be in a regular class next year."

"He's a little slow but I hired a private tutor as soon as I saw his scores."

"My aunt says she'll grow out of it."

"These public schools are over-crowded and he's too shy to speak up."

Labels change as the seasons come and go until you finally realize that *smart social worker* is an oxymoron, though you want to believe their pasted-on cheer is as positive as they promise. When President Ford passed PS 94–142, no money went along with it. This means that the public schools are obliged to lie or pay for extra services, and allowing that they know how hard it is and will continue to be, I choke on what some of the teachers serve up. Young and sincere and so full of clichés they could as easily be Victorian farm wives who stand proudly behind jars of peach preserves with sweat on their foreheads and smiles on their faces, talking about prizes at the county fair. As much use to me. At least you can spread peach preserves on whole wheat bread and nourish yourself.

I'm not one to give up, but early on, I learned support is something that goes best with long line girdles and D-cup bras. I figured I'd find a role model on my own, having accepted none of the jargon that crams the airwaves and bores the hell out of the average person.

CHAPTER 16

I can't forget my upbringing. Our dinner table had a single rule—if you took it, you ate it. Or else. Even our family legends appear clean cut—they move along in a clear direction up to this very moment. Our family philosophy fit in one sentence: Clean your plate, pipe down, and sit still. It was a war of the mouth, and my father was in charge. I spent years waiting to leave. Finally, I moved up, away from my parents, on to college and a profession. Seven years of part-time jobs, stops and starts, and then I graduated. An English major prepared me for a world long gone, when dinner parties weren't overtaken by shop talk, by either worrying about or bragging about your kids. When, for awhile, we all had futures, when falling snow felt cozy, and I could walk on New Year's Eve to a party up the street. Not running boards and rumble seats, not that far back. Oh God, the past.

I still live in this Detroit suburb which surprises my husband because I've always hated cars, the new models, the insides, the gadgets, the hard sell, the mysteries of speed. Most of all, I hate the long conversations about Ford and GM, even glimpses of sleek car races on TV. They torch Porsches here. Foreign car is a dirty word, akin to *Arab* anywhere but Dearborn—and a new BMW makes its owner a traitor.

But I could live anywhere and these same men would bore me to death with automotive details. All of America is in love with speed and chrome. few places are uglier than a parking lot. Rich or poor, neighborhoods that hold two and three cars per family are blighted. Actually, Detroit appealed to me with that one exception, because I learned early not to expect too much. So we stayed right here, grad school in Ann Arbor, a lot of aborted plans to see Europe. It all sped by, and my dreams of travel with it. I think Paris is out, though they take care of their old in France. Our next big move may be to a home.

If you're vulnerable, you're out clutching a list of dead ends in your frail hand. All on official paper. And that's what hurts most. All these promises and what they've done to me and my husband. "I won't do anything you don't want to do," is a line with a little more sophistication, and I'll admit I once almost fell for that ploy in the steamy back seat of a '49 Ford.

Don't let me waste any more time digressing. I'm an old woman. People think it's a compliment if they say, "You're not old," as if you were blind too at sixty-eight. Most women have given into the sag of life by now or put their all into hair color and a strident laugh. I should have grandchildren, but I have Isobel in Tokyo, John Baxter checking out ecology in Alaska, and an unmarried daughter in town. That daughter, Jenny Grier, can't seem to find herself.

Melody has been in supported employment for fourteen years. At first, she ran a mimeograph machine, slowly and deliberately. The colored buttons weren't hard to learn and the machine jammed for everybody, not just her. She waited patiently for the repairman. A full week for Melody is four hours a day and she is rarely late. She has a pretty smile and tight hug. I tell her story sometimes failing to include what that hug got her into. Oh, she didn't mind the mimeo machine or delivering letters of complaint. It was office politics that got to her. How could she understand the gossip? Hell, I'm Summa cum Laude, and schoolhouse infighting never made sense to me.

CHAPTER 17

What I've lost, what I long for is what I expected to continue—the thread that connected me to Isobel. I can't imagine her in Kyoto with no job and a man I've never met. How can Isobel, the feminist in our family, succumb to a place where women live in another century, still? How can Isobel, who spent her adolescence attached to our recliner with a book in her lap, never far from a coffeepot, sip tea on the floor from a cup without handles?

Looking back, I lost Isobel gradually. It began with a boyfriend whose motives were clear to us but never to her. She was enchanted by Grover—a big talker and unfailingly polite: "Your parents are devoted to Melody. How did they do it all? With three other kids?" He was astounded by Melody's *independence* as well; but what he was really saying was something else entirely. He avoided sitting near her, preferring a sudden shift to the patio (Melody was afraid of mosquitoes) or even an untimely trip to the bathroom while he thought of a new ploy. At least that's the way it seemed to me. His greetings were perfunctory; his birthday cards on time; but his eyes never connected to Melody's or mine. Occasionally his real feelings surfaced: "Haven't you told us about your bus driver one time too many, Melody?" He had little gestures, glancing back and forth to his watch at family dinners; a few too many "Yes, sir's" for Charlie. His was a confidence based on book learning. He was a psych major; and he could make the complex simple and call it truth. Grover went out of his way to seem interested in what had become our Special Ed library. He read the two Josh Greenfield books; and then assured me, quoting from the text, that Melody was nowhere near as bad as Noah and there would surely be a place for her, a program. His pronouncements were pompous and Isobel swallowed them all. He was a devout Catholic and truly believed that Melody was a "gift." Then they got engaged, but he was too cheap for a ring. Things continued for a year or so; and she finally came to her senses. Instead of putting him through grad school, she went on with her own education. It wasn't long before he eloped with a girl who lived up the street and considered him a "good catch," the woman's movement having passed her by too. Charlie took me out for ice cream to celebrate Grover's departure.

Our jubilation was not to last because Isobel is gone now and we don't even know who she's living with. A man with a Fulbright? I keep remembering her baby book with every birthday party until she was ten described in a paragraph with a photo next to it. Her footprints. A lock of her hair. Her charcoal drawings framed in the hallway. Charlie did them up in his workshop. And all those children's books, hardbacks, inscribed by me, with long messages after the children were asleep; and Charlie, too, in that recliner. Isobel left those books on her bedroom shelf; her clothes in the closet, except for a black dress and a pin striped suit we bought her for graduation. "The books can stay. Why don't you donate them to Melody's school?" she said.

The distance grew longer, faster then. First Isobel forgot my birthday. Then Charlie's. Then we got a belated Christmas card. "The phone lines were tied up," she said. Then there were no cards and no excuses. So we are left with the family album. Her report cards make the book bulge. Isobel was a straight A student.

CHAPTER 18

My memories come in fits and starts. One happy summer, before adolescence hit us hard, I was weeding lettuce and drifting with the insects. It was June 1st. Melody never missed a summer camp and the leaders wore her out and gave her a lot to talk about. I alternated driving mornings with another mother, so I was free this particular morning. Melody had packed her own lunch the night before; a sack full of Trail Mix and a juice box with one of those miniature straws. And after the car backed out, Charlie and I went for at least ten minutes of silence together before we both fell asleep in the lawn chairs.

Camp has no P.T.A. You pay for camp and the leaders are happier than classroom teachers are, at least it seemed that way. Charlie and I could even go back to bed on rainy mornings. So this is how other people live? Those summers with Charlie were hard to let go, and I'm not talking about sunshine and lettuce leaves.

We could have read Yeats to each other, "The Lake Isle of Inisfree where peace comes dropping slow;" we could have squeezed lemonade from fresh lemons; but we stayed an inch apart in those lawn chairs, the kind you find on ships, deck chairs really, and we talked neither about the past, nor the weeks to come.

Here in Michigan, men go fishing to find peace like that, away from automobile exhausts and phones; but they have to get on the lake before the sun comes up and wait quietly in a boat. This idyll of ours was easier, and we could count on it—then. When we were a family, when we all lived under the same roof and hadn't admitted our mistakes to each other; before Isobel's airplane left for Kyoto and John Baxter bought land in Juno. Before Jenny Grier enrolled for her first degree at Wayne State.

CHAPTER 19

It was Sunday, the year before Melody's graduation from high school with a "special diploma." We moved in and out of some optimistic circles then. Words like "independent" and "normalize" were part of the picture; and for awhile we listened to the people who mouthed them. Charlie was propped up in bed reading the *Detroit Free Press*, and I was pretending to be asleep when he crunched up part of the paper and cursed loud enough to wake the dead. Naturally I sat up. By then he was in the bathroom with the door shut. I restored the page to its original form, at least enough to read the article—a long piece with photographs about two retarded adults getting married. The mother was all smiles and the happy couple was standing together holding hands.

Included in the text was a long explanation of the melding of the two families, the jobs of all concerned, and many references to the joys to come for one and all. I didn't read the whole thing, but I recognized the bride and knew her family had plenty of money and the influence that goes with it. The bride was a greeter at Wal-Mart, and her husband had bagged groceries at the Kroger in Royal Oak for years. They planned to live in a condo near the grocery and she would take public transportation to her job. It was a long article, as I said, and every detail of their lives seemed to be worked out. An agency would be in charge of helping them keep a checkbook and a social worker would visit them twice a week. They would take cooking lessons in their spare time.

I didn't say a word when Charlie came out of the bathroom, but I didn't get out of bed either. I had a pile of laundry I didn't want to face. Melody was a bed wetter, and things accumulate. I never pushed that task off on the other children. I did it myself. Occasionally there was still some pleasure in folding clean towels with the smell and the heat of the dryer lingering on their surface. But not that Sunday.

Why did I ever imagine I could live outside history? At a time when the homeless fill our cities, where communities cannot protect us from each other, where neither schools nor libraries are the sanctuaries they once were, only a fool would expect protection. I was that fool.

Last night Charlie and I watched *The Verdict* for the fourth time in as many years, my feet tucked behind his back, and a pillow under my head. He sat there staring at the TV screen: "We are, none of us, protected. We just have to go on." The words came once again from Paul Newman's mouth. He plays a seedy attorney who sips whiskey with his breakfast donut perched on a pinball machine. Newman's attorney is fighting the Catholic Church and the medical profession, and at first it looks like he doesn't have a chance. But he does. The movie takes place in Boston, and we live in Detroit, not so far away, I hope. Because it's a chance I want too; yet sometimes I feel in that movie is the only place I'll find it. Bobby Short died yesterday, and I learned this morning that the

Plaza has been turned into condominiums. To top it off, rumor has it that the Fulton Fish Market is moving to the Bronx.

CHAPTER 20

Isobel Speaks

I came to Japan with no thought of learning more Japanese or staying very long. I was living with a man on a Fulbright; and God knows he knew which strings need pulling and how to write a grant proposal. He wanted me at his side. I have my mother's eyes and hair; and my sisters say I'm just as stubborn. So I packed a bag and left my family behind—each one in the middle of a speech on why I shouldn't go. Melody was the only one in tears, but the look on my mother's face almost made me reconsider. Two teachers in one family are enough, and what else could I do with a stopgap degree? A Master's in comparative lit and no prospects. True, I spoke French and knew a few erotic phrases in Italian; but then I hadn't even read Mishima or that Japanese Nobel Prize winner who committed suicide too. Imagine how I fit in. Tall with red hair and that kind of fair skin that sunburns in five minutes.

Japan is not the point, but you have to start somewhere; and this was the first time I was free of Melody, so it seemed like a real beginning. There I was with no project and a stack of paperbacks my father gave me, Berkley Medallion novels he bought when they were $1.25 each—Japanese novels in translation written after World War II that he bought in the early sixties complete with dust and bookworms. I was alone all day with little desire to explore Kyoto. I wanted to breathe. Sure I wrote letters to my mother and read hers over and over; but there were no family pictures on these walls. The man with the Fulbright seemed happy with his prospects. He liked being in control.

Kyoto, saved from destruction because of history! I was not yet ready to meet what its unnamed streets had to offer, unable to use the opportunity to explore the fabled beauty of its temples and museums. Reading instead of cherry blossom viewing. Thus seeing secondhand moonlight that illuminated the blossoms until it became a presence in itself, albeit on the printed page.

"You lead a vicarious life, Isobel. Even here," The Fulbright scholar told me. "Just like your mother," he continued.

"Better than no life at all," I thought to myself as I drifted further into a bio of Mishima—fascinated by the grandmother's sick room where he grew up. I know better than to argue with a man in a foreign country. I didn't have a job or a ticket back home. Yet.

I never thought I'd get this far. Loose tea, Saki, and this Habachi in the middle of the floor; and I'm still cold. In college we drank coffee every winter afternoon in the student center, with gray slush waiting for us outside the dirty brick building. The streets were frozen with hidden patches of ice, far from the fabled snow of a New England winter, January in Detroit passed into a March thaw and we waited for spring.

We lived in an old hotel—the men on one floor above the women; the walls were hospital green and the proctor's desk, heavy and dark, stood where the corridors formed an "L" just a few steps from the elevators. There was no real curfew. No lights out unless your roommate forced you or bribed you and that was rare. We learned to sleep with the lights on. No glamour, no soft pillows or homemade quilts. We used what was given us—free, scratchy gray wool blankets. Nothing like this futon. There was no drift to it. I had to be flat out exhausted to sleep in that dorm.

My trip over here was smoothed out by the man with the Fulbright who ran interference for me in every way he could. He arrived first, found an apartment, bought a bag of rice and a futon, and was waiting for me at Baggage Claim. There was a solitary cat on the curb when we closed the apartment door, and I longed to lie down with him on that futon forever. His laptop was the only connection I wanted with the outside world, and it sat on the other end of the room on his suitcase.

Kyoto bears the extremes of the seasons. The summers are hot and humid and the winters so bitter that the people of Kyoto believe that the cold "comes out of the ground," or so they say. He wrapped the futon around me and I felt captured. I had waited a long time for him and this room and the pleasure I expect to find.

I don't know what my father told John Baxter about sex, but I can tell you my mother left no stone unturned when it came to birth control. We knew the devices, their history, their flaws. She started when I was eight with color-coded charts. The stick figures red. I examined a diaphragm before I was 12 years old. Jenny Grier knew that tubes could be tied and untied before she even owned a training bra. By the time we were 14, we had a shelf full of well-worn paperbacks on Planned Parenthood in the room we shared, and a bibliography on a pink Xerox sheet.

My mother went way beyond the usual fears of pregnancy, way past the honesty of the sexual revolution. "My God, mother; I'm not even going steady!" We thought she had gone around the bend until one of Melody's friends got pregnant during her first year of high school and became a double burden. When Melody herself was assaulted, we realized that it was Melody our mother was worried about. As usual.

What is the upshot of it all? It's control, all right. Jenny Grier, though she has never talked to me about it and wouldn't be caught dead with a short haircut and comfortable shoes, is a lesbian as sure as my name is Isobel Anderson. Isobel Ward Anderson, to fit into this family.

CHAPTER 21

Problems accumulate. It's a matter of history. Accidents in Melody's underpants that are no accident. It is common with the retarded, who have limited means to cry for help, unconscious, of course. Enuresis, a fancy word, and when it happens in a child over five, it's a serious thing, a warning. These labels are supposed to help me as I clean her up. But at age 35, it's merely stress and the other label no longer fits. Everything is like that—confusing—once the mind quits growing somewhere between age ten and twelve.

Anyway, sometimes motherhood amounts to cleaning up shit and then scrubbing the particles from underneath your nails, while remembering to take a breath, and then another, and go on. Last year my friend who took to drink after the PTSA no longer worked had a stroke, a little one, a T.I.A. She forgot to take those breaths, she forgot to rest, and she ended up on that sliding board that moves into a machine. She likened it to gunfire or the sound of a staple gun. She had a lot of time to think in that hospital room, a week, in fact. Now, she has to take a maroon capsule morning and night, and she thanks the powers that be that she's still here.

The past meets the present in layers and spirals, and all the details I've forgotten, or tried to forget, return. Melody's job now, when her job coach isn't there keeping an eye on things, is not what we'd like it to be. Two hotel waiters tease a retarded busboy until he is riled up; the supervisor takes a cigarette break while another boy has a seizure; and Melody is too scared to tell us until weeks pass. The hotel windows are steamed up as I remember the place the day I came down to see for myself what showed on the outside.

Melody sometimes refuses to go to work, only she won't say why. Instead, she picks the scabs on her legs until they are a sea of Band-Aids. It's an old problem and I don't care if you label it OCD or nerves. The label does nothing to help me, and Melody finds a time and a place to secretly draw blood until I walk around with Neosporin in my purse and pockets, and carefully remove the flesh colored strips before her bath. Bath time with all those bubbles up to her chin—her delight in blowing them away from her mouth. I'm babying her, but why not? Isobel sent her a post card from Kyoto showing the baths there with huge rocks and rising steam. Melody carries it into the bathroom, props it on the clothes hamper until she trails it and a towel back to her room. I let her put on the new Band-Aids herself and by Friday, she finally tells us what happened at work. We call the job coach and, this once, miraculously, the waiter is fired. There is a lull in my life, then.

I have, in fact, taken up knitting, which seems to be the rage in Huntington Woods. There are even groups of women who descend on Starbucks and Barnes & Noble with thick yarn and fat needles but they don't drink much coffee. Neither do I.

I have holes in my memory, but some details keep Melody's story lined up in my head. She was always awkward. Ungainly. Not unlike most of her classmates. Neurological damage often can travel to other parts of the body and it does. Once, when she was mainstreamed into a PE class, oh, she was at least thirteen, she asked to sit out the basketball practice. There, on the last step of the bleachers, she found three other girls who had been together for a few weeks (we never knew why; we could only surmise) and a frail girl on crutches. Well, Melody never asked to return to practice and the coaches ignored her. Weeks went by with her the fifth wheel on the bench. I eventually got a call from the Special Ed teacher; I remember it was a Tuesday around 4:00 PM. She said Melody's friend had just told her that for weeks, the tiny mob of three, had thrown Melody's parka over the top bleacher and when Melody ran back to retrieve it, they spit on her. This happened every day and the coaches could not have helped but see it, but looked the other way. This Tuesday, the girls had talked her into removing her underpants.

"Why didn't you tell me?" the Special Education teacher asked Melody.

"I just knew the coaches would help me!" came the reply.

Another time Melody stayed with my cousin in Harrisville, Michigan on lake Huron. She'd been invited more than once, and she was fourteen by then. It was a mild summer. It seemed safe. The beach below, two blocks from a movie, the town filled with retirees, the library remodeled, and the librarian, maternal. Melody liked those coffee table books with glossy photographs in color, and not much text.

My cousin had two boys, ordinary boys, polite to their mother most of the time. Up early. Full of energy. We called every evening to see how things were going, but Melody couldn't explain much. She couldn't tell us why but her feet were bleeding as she emerged from walking in blackberry brambles, sweating, unable to talk. What happened? We didn't find out for a long time. And even then, we couldn't blame my cousin. She treated Melody the same way she treated her own boys. She merely yelled at them when they missed the toilet and peed on the tile. Melody watched. My cousin expected her sons to wash the dishes and Melody helped them dry. A lot of crockery shattered that summer. My cousin's patience wore thin.

I know how irritating Melody's questions, repeated over and over, can be. They can, on occasion, make me shake. And when you're not used to her questions, it's harder. I can only imagine my cousin in my place. "What would you like for breakfast, dear?" I know what Melody must have said, "Raisin Bran, please." She likes to pick out the raisins and line them up—saving the best till last and eating them, one by one.

Such silly rituals delight her and they comfort me because she will look up and smile after each bite. I can't help but smile back. I also like driving her to the doctor because we play the same CDs—*Chicago, West Side Story*, and soon we're there. At such times, we're satisfied with the music and each other. Anyway, my cousin told Melody: "We can't afford Raisin Bran," and ladled her up a glob of oatmeal. Melody can feel resentment. She's had a lifetime to develop her skill. Who really knows how that resentment leaked out? But she came home then; and, as usual, things were worse, not better.

CHAPTER 22

When I look back and consider what flashes through my head, I have to feel grateful for all the good that has come my way; from the Japanese poems Isobel used to send me on rice paper, regularly, to the favors my father-in-law did for us up until the very day he died. When Melody was four, we took her to Chicago on the train for his wake. We arrived, all six of us, with scarves over our mouths and homemade mittens shielding our hands from that bitter wind that whipped around the tall buildings and almost blew us into the church.

Charlie and his brothers all had too much to drink and wouldn't stop playing "Can You Top This?" with family stories of way back when Charlie was a Quiz Kid and won a Cocker Spaniel puppy causing his family to be evicted. "You couldn't just take the savings bond," his brother slapped his knee. Their father looked for that same dog years later, all night through an ice storm, and then came home alone, distraught. It is always winter in these stories. The brothers nodded and coughed while Charlie told about the time he backed his mother's car out of the driveway when he was supposed to be watching his little brothers. Charlie was fourteen. He knocked the pickets off the fence, one by one, and was edging toward a porch pillar when his brother Vincent stopped him: "Think fast", Vin said and Charlie ran inside for a sprinkling can, doused water on the pickets while Vin held them steady. They froze like glue, but in the morning … and here the story tapers off in my memory because I am watching Melody and the casket and remembering that I didn't have breakfast. The tale ends, though, with my father-in-law beating the crap out of both boys.

I felt warm, just listening, with my family close by and Melody in her uncle's lap. So different was all that talk and adventure and rage and worry from my tight-lipped life as an only child. I grew up, often speechless, waiting year after year for escape from my father's iron hand and hot temper. "I don't know how you stand it!" Charlie's Dad said at the first sight of Melody's classmates in a school program, so many of them at once; the wheelchairs, the unfocused eyes, and the nervous laughter. Forever after, he did all he could to help us stand it. He sent money, and he was not a rich man. A giant doll that bowled us over, a tiny porcelain figurine that I still keep on my dresser, and Christmas cards the size of a loose leaf folder. He fancied himself Santa Claus and arrived every Christmas to sleep in the twin bed in John Baxter's room. All those Januarys dragged by and no matter how white the snow, the days were gray as soon as he left. He taught the kids to play "Hearts" and laughed when one of them stuck him with the Queen. Somehow he fit Melody into the game until I could whisk her away to help me bake cookies. Every afternoon during Christmas week, we ate so many cookies so fast that it was hard to finish a bowl of stew at suppertime. You can't replace people. Not those who tell the truth and then do something about it. I miss him horribly.

CHAPTER 23

So, with each trial, we ended worse off than when we began until the boarding school fiasco, and then with no one to blame but ourselves, thinking we could escape statistics. Bad luck, we told ourselves at the time. The abuse percentages now included us. The toughest part of that experience wasn't the money, tuition, wardrobe, plane fares home and fares to visit; it was Melody's fragility that would never change now. Again statistics, and this time, we no longer felt above them. A second psychotic break is likely to follow the first.

We are careful now, even more wary of the experts and their recommendations. Charlie saw through the slogans and the arguments immediately; but I wanted to believe until the day they closed the retardation centers, under-funded supported employment programs, and pushed independent living as an answer. Much cheaper—the bottom line.

We have adapted to these changes by providing a room of her own for Melody with a connecting bath and hallway, and a recreation program at the Jewish Community Center. It is called "Very Special People." Though we are not Jews, there is no discrimination and I will never stop being grateful for that fact. I also hired a trainer temporarily for all of us and we took exercise moderately, daily, and it helped. Walking wasn't enough.

The people at the Center, from the coffee man to the ex-surgical nurse who greets us every weekday at the front desk, were never insincere. Full of decency. Always there taking complaints from others with grace, answering phones and questions, and never saying, "I know how you feel." That phrase makes me want to curse in public and scream in private, in the shower, with the door shut.

Life has become a process of loss, of expecting far less and learning the meaning of real humility, of always guarding against using a scapegoat; though there were plenty of fools around to fill that bill. Each one has "the answer" and a book they found it in. I listened and, at last, I learned to keep my mouth shut until I could laugh with Charlie or write a letter to a friend. I had e-mail now and was consoled by it.

We read everything but self-help books now—classics, comedies, President Clinton's favorite mystery writer, Walter Mosley, most of his work, twice. We had unplugged the TV for a while until September 11th shocked us back to grieve for my favorite city. The sight of President Bush with his bull horn, in a pile of rubble with his arm around a fireman made me tear up and cry until the skin around my eyes was raw. For that brief spell, when the smoking towers and the workers digging up the dead made us open our checkbooks and our hearts, we realized that our life was far better than no life at all.

The Huntington Woods library is no longer quiet. Computers and audiotapes are fast becoming a bigger draw than books; a fact that makes me furious.

"The best suburban library in the county, and it's not good enough for you, Elizabeth! You need more medicine," my husband said, popping a coke can at 6:00 A.M. on a day when the air conditioning failed.

"Take a look in the mirror," I whispered, walking away.

As for our children, pretending and rationalizing became their style. Their so-called independence is an illusory escape from the present and the future, from us, and from Melody. Sometimes I have to concentrate hard not to run too, from Charlie and my friends. And, I'm not talking about other cities or countries far away. I'm talking about leaving my car and crossing the freeway some Saturday night in dark clothes when the traffic is steady. I'm talking about leaving without a suitcase or a purse to anchor me. You see I am not as brave as Charlie or as sane as my four children.

Melody's response to Isobel's departure surprised me. "Who's going to brush my hair?" she teared up. Isobel had done so much for her, but it was this surefire part of the morning routine that worried Melody most. Sometimes I brushed her hair then too, just to calm myself down, before bed, some afternoons too; but it was Isobel's brushing that mattered.

"Isobel's coming home next year. On the plane. With my Christmas presents. On the Plane, Mom!"

And how can I tell her about the likelihood of that? I don't even try.

CHAPTER 24

After all that decorating and my pleasure in controlling the colors in this house—at least as vivid as the hot pinks of my former classroom—after my morning walk (today in the rain), I am starring at this laptop on a desk free of clutter and wondering about all the space in my life. This keyboard, the tiny green light, the mail truck voice reassuring in its regularity, and finally, an empty screen waiting for my words. With Melody back at work, I can write family letters now (not to John Baxter, who has no computer); not to Isabel (who could use the one belonging to the man with the Fulbright, but doesn't.) No, my letters are to Jenny Grier—my closest yet farthest child, probably sleeping in her rented room after a night of lifting heavy trays and measuring out her smiles. It's two-for-one, but Jenny Grier always responds, and her talk is never small.

Our conversation has stretched out over the years. It began after her first Master's Degree, long before I retired. Then it was two-for-one in her corner: interesting observations of what buildings were left at WSU, what professors were still alive. Charlie was included in these letters for they were written after Melody was asleep, and the two of us could rest in our easy chairs. We already knew that Webster Hall had been imploded and some enterprising graduate was selling off the remaining bricks to raise funds for the university. But hearing from her that both seventy and eighty West Warren made room for a parking lot brought silence and a wave of nostalgia. A studio on the third floor of seventy West, the most down-at-the-heels of the two buildings, now existed only on a page of black and white photographs in our album and in the far recesses of our memories. Charlie's best friend had lived there, and his parties were legendary.

Anyway, such longing for our college years and critic teachers filled some of our happier evenings. We fancied ourselves closer to Jenny Grier than we were. The miracle of email. Back and forth, our words: Charlie with a literary quote, and Jenny Grier with a question about his gardenia bush that brought forth a gush of floral commentary designed to entice her back to our hammock where she spent her summers before everybody's adolescence exploded. Nothing was a haven then, not the hallway window seats, the back porch glider, Charlie's basement workshop and certainly not that hammock, fixed in sunlight, rotted by rain until it collapsed one July afternoon—leaving Jenny's behind on the ground and her feet in the air. "Librarians raised me," she once said, referring to being pushed aside by Melody, "But for awhile I thought I had a place here!" The next day she scheduled sleepovers, with military regularity, and no return engagements. Jenny Grier had a lot of girlfriends.

At first I had faith in Special Education, and then came the light bulb episode. After that I was angry enough to want a separate bedroom, but since we didn't have one, my rage eventually grew loose, the pain in my chest went away, and I was left with a flutter.

The doctor called it an irregular heartbeat and I sat in the sun that fall near the asparagus stalks Charlie was so proud of with nothing on my mind but asparagus haze.

The light bulb episode began as a game with all four children as players: Anything you can do, I can do better. For once, Melody thought she would win: "I can make that light bulb move. I can make that light bulb turn blue." The others laughed, but Isobel asked how. Melody leaned back on my bedroom carpet and closed her eyes. The children had been playing on the floor while Jenny Grier and I folded jockey shorts. Melody went on, "I do it every day. I have my own little room now and I can watch the light bulb as long as I want."

As she told us the story of her separation from the group (a collection of six and seven year olds who weren't quite dumb enough to fit EMR, as the testing showed it that year, not belligerent enough to be classified as behavior disordered, and not smart enough for a regular class), who were part of an experiment with a teacher fresh from Ypsilanti with a handful of M&M's and total trust in behavior modification without understanding what it was. The teacher's lesson plans back-fired and Melody became more and more distracted until she was locked in a windowless room with a desk and a light bulb.

I saw this teacher the next day, red in the face, with a Special Ed Supervisor who didn't want to give Melody a Kleenex: "I want Melody to ask for one herself, because it would muddy our scientific observation." She seemed proud to see Melody fidgeting, yes, distracted; and she was fully confident that isolation would work wonders! Melody appeared to be choking on snot. I can't remember what I said or did that morning, but that afternoon, Charlie was late for supper and his face was flushed. He took me aside and told me that the supervisor had called his school and taken him out of class to say, "Mr. Anderson, we can't deal with your angry wife."

"I told the supervisor to expect me before four, and if she thought I was any less angry, she was sadly mistaken."

We ate fast that night. The children washed the dishes and the sound of broken glass didn't bother me one bit, I could have added to the melee, if I hadn't had Charlie to hold me back. He knows the right music to play. At first, Charlie just listened to his Ornette Coleman cassette. He moved his sweaty glass from the coaster to his lips and took a long swallow. I kept on talking, though my voice was lower and I hesitated as I watched his hand replace the glass.

"Shut up, Elizabeth. There is no answer for us. Some things are better left to saxophones! It does no good to cry."

"I'm … not … crying."

He took my hand and we moved on to our bedroom. There is a place near his arm where my body lies touching his—my foot across his ankle. He has always been in charge of the stereo, fixing his own concert with John Coltrane following Charlie Parker. Sometimes a whole hour of Billie Holiday when her music joins the drift of memories and a dream emerges where the flower in her hair floats and disappears into the darkness of a Harlem night. All that is left is a spotlight illuminating her microphone. Her ghost deserts me then. When I wake up, Billie's words are still with us. Charlie moves closer:

He wears high draped pants; stripes are really yellow.
But when he starts in to love me, he's so fine and mellow.

At such times I forget Melody exists and the only light left burning is a single bulb in the bathroom. Saxophones rule.

Biography

Recipient of a 2001 Yaddo Writers' Fellowship, June Akers Seese is also the author of two novels, *Is This What Other Women Feel Too?* and *What Waiting Really Means*, plus a collection of short fiction, *James Mason and the Walk-In Closet*, all published by Dalkey Archive Press. Her short stories have appeared in *Witness, Carolina Quarterly*, and *South Caroline Review*, and they are collected in three chapbooks funded by the Georgia Council for the Arts: *Near Occasions of Sin, Claudia and a Long Line of Women*, and *My Affairs are in Order/All Those Men are Dead Now*. Mrs. Seese teaches The Memoir: Reading It and Writing It at Callanwolde Fine Arts Center in Atlanta, Georgia. *A Nurse Can Go Anywhere and Collected Stories* is forthcoming in 2008.

978-0-595-44661-2
0-595-44661-2

CPSIA information can be obtained
at www.ICGtesting.com
Printed in the USA
JSHW021049280623
43899JS00005B/43